THE
BOOK
OF
LANEY

Also by the Author

Echolocation
I Am Holding Your Hand

THE
BOOK
OF
LANEY

a novel

Myfanwy Collins

LACEWING BOOKS
INDIANAPOLIS

Lacewing Books
an imprint of Engine Books
PO Box 44167
Indianapolis, IN 46244
lacewingbooks.org

Printed in the United States of America

10   9   8   7   6   5   4   3   2   1

ISBN: 978-1-938126-28-4

Library of Congress Control Number: 2014944274

I dedicate this book to my sisters, Michaela and Cathy. No matter how far apart we may be, we will always be together. I love you.

My Story Does Not Start Here

Here and now I am in this place far away from my home. Here, with the cold wind blowing down from the north and the stars piercing through the cloudless sky. Here I am.

But my story does not start here.

My story starts months ago and hundreds of miles south of where I am now. My story starts in the place I used to call home. My story starts with violence and heartbreak.

My story starts with a vision.

Mark is up ahead of me, pushing to the back of the bus. The light smearing through the windows is a dull toothache of yellow. I rub a hand over my eyes to clear them. It's my hand. It's not my hand. I feel what it feels and when I look at it, I recognize it, but I don't know it to really be mine. But I'm here. I'm still here. There is nowhere else I could be and this is real. One kid starts screaming and Mark points his machete at the kid and tells him that if he doesn't shut his face, he's next. It could be a scene from a movie or a game but it's real. It's real. I keep saying, "This is real. This is real," to remind myself that I'm in this place with Mark.

Mark looks back at me over his shoulder, "Come on, dude. Let's get this party started." He laughs and so I laugh, too, but I don't really feel like laughing. I want to lie down. I want to run away. I'm not sure what I'm doing and why I'm doing it. I hear moaning behind me and Mark catches me as I flinch. "Don't worry about them, bro,"

Mark says, indicating the people in the seats behind me. "They ain't going nowhere." He's trying to sound badass.

I take a step and then another step. People are crying, sniffling, sucking in their snot. The windows have steamed up and the air now smells of blood. Someone is praying softly. I turn toward the voice. I see Mariah, her eyes shut, hands clasped. Her fingernails are painted black. I've thought about her sometimes. What it'd be like to be with her. To touch her skin. Her hands are like whispers across her paper when she takes down notes. We have Geometry together. Had. I mean had. There will be no more Geometry after this.

Even though she was a cheerleader, she smiled at me once in the hall, said, "Hi." I saw her playing on the monkey bars at the park once. She was with a couple of little kids she must've been babysitting. Her body moved easily from bar to bar, her hands propelling her thin arms forward. But here we are now and her eyes meet mine and I lift the hand with my knife in it, raise my arm right up over my head. I know she's frightened but she won't let her eyes show it. I want her to show her fear. It would be easier for me to kill her then.

"Aren't you scared to die?" I ask her. I will stab her. I will hurt her. I might even kill her. She doesn't deserve to live. The pain.

"Please don't hurt me, West," she says.

She knows my name. She said my name. West.

"Please," she says. She isn't even crying.

Mark screams back to me, "Bro! Cut her and get on with it." He's busy and laughing. People are freaking out, pushing each other over seats. Pushing each other down.

Within the swirl of the chaos, I remain still.

"Lie down and pretend you're dead," I whisper to her. "It'll all be over soon."

She does as she's told and I keep walking, pushing into the mess.

"Did you get her?" Mark calls back to me and I nod. My hands are shaking. I look down at them and see the veins sticking out on top. I see the familiar color of the skin. The odd freckle between thumb *and forefinger.*

The vision ends there with the realization that what I've seen doesn't belong to me. I know those hands. Those shaking hands weren't really my hands. I'm Laney Kates and I'm a girl. Those hands belonged to a boy. Those hands belonged to West.

Those hands were my brother's hands.

I'm not on a bus. I'm in a room in a house far away from the home I once shared with my mother and my brother. My story starts with a vision. Within a vision within a vision within a vision, all tunneling backward in time, all reflecting forward into my brain. The hands were part of the vision and within that vision is the truth and the way forward, but we cannot go forward without first going back.

One

Winter came on quick. The tree frogs quit singing me to sleep early in October. By November there was snow. From December on, I felt ice in everything I did, moving across my words as I spoke them, covering over my breath. Felt it snaking up through my nostrils and into my brain, crusting over thought. Ice was everywhere, crystalline and hard-edged.

In January, the thermometer marked the freezing but Mrs. Coughlin sat on her deck, a loaded BB gun across her lap. She was ready to take down some squirrels. I watched her from the vine-covered, chain-link fence that separated our two properties. I coughed so that she'd notice me and not be spooked and shoot me. She turned her narrow head and nodded, wire-rimmed glasses pinching her nose. I waved and she nodded again, looking down at the gun this time. "They should have used one of these on your brother," she said, widening her eyes for emphasis. "Except a real one, with bullets." She turned the gun in my direction and mocked shooting at me so that I'd get the picture.

Might seem like a pretty hostile move coming from an old lady like Mrs. Coughlin, but I'd come to expect stuff like this from her. One minute she was holding out her hand to help me and the next minute she was pulling it away. Still, her hand seemed like the only hand anyone had ever held out to me, even if it did sometimes have a gun in it.

I turned my head toward her bird feeders. Mrs. Coughlin may have been crazy but I guess she had a point. She was talking about how the victims should've used guns. The teachers. The students. The kids I went to school with. She was talking about how my mother should've used a gun. She was talking about how those who were murdered should've used guns. Maybe she also meant their families should've used guns. Maybe she meant the police. Maybe she meant everyone—society and whatever—should've used guns. Maybe she meant I should've used a gun. Everyone should've used guns to kill my brother and his best friend. Especially the people who died. They should've defended themselves. But they didn't. They couldn't.

Those murdered and wounded were unarmed and unsuspecting. They were innocent.

Though she'd lowered her gun, Mrs. Coughlin was still watching me when I turned my eyes back to her. "Yup," I said. I couldn't argue with her. Someone should've shot West. Maybe I should've, but I didn't have a gun. I don't even believe in guns because I'm a pacifist, like the Dalai Lama. I have been ever since I wrote an essay about him in sixth grade. I believe that the only reason there are wars is because there are poor people to fight them and greedy people who want to make money off the fighting. When you give people no other option but to work as a soldier so that they can feed their family and when people in power care more about how much money they have than about everyone having a decent life, then there will always be wars. And even though I'm poor, I will never fight in a war. I'm not brave. It would be easier for me to starve than face death. I'm quiet. I like to read books and think. I am not a fighter.

But Mrs. Coughlin was a fighter. The world as we knew it had been wiped out and replaced with its ugly, angry twin. It was like we were living in a mirror reflection of our lives except that everything we once believed was no longer true. And all of this devastation was totally avoidable. It wasn't because of some flood or hurricane or act of God. No. It was because West and Mark had acted as judge and jury and they'd decided the fate of those they believed had wronged them.

What happened was a catastrophe. It was a bloodbath. It was everything. But I wasn't there, and so I've had to patch together the story. This is what I have from reports and rumors. This is what I have from my own experience and recollection. This is what I know. Here we go.

The varsity boys' basketball team and their cheerleaders, coaches, water boys, and chaperones were waiting on the idling bus in the school parking lot. They were headed out to a neighboring town for what was meant to be the game of the year. The team they were scheduled to play was our biggest rival. The bus was filled with crazy energy. Loud music. Empty water bottles thrown here and there. Someone had brought a huge balloon and was bouncing it around. The cheerleading coach, Mrs. DeMato, was furiously trying to grab the thing and deflate it because she was worried about latex allergies and the no balloons allowed on school property policy.

Even so, she was laughing.

Everyone was laughing.

Good times.

When they entered the bus, West and Mark were dressed in identical camouflage outfits. They'd both been growing beards but were not yet men, so their facial hair was sparse, patchy. My mother's boyfriend, Archie, had teased West about his beard for weeks before the incident, cackling over the hilarity of my brother's peach fuzz. He nicknamed West "Fuzzy." Each time Archie called him Fuzzy, West lifted an imaginary gun and pretended to shoot him, which only made Archie laugh harder—not so funny in retrospect.

Their faces where covered in camo paint. They looked ready for paintball. They looked like kids. They didn't look tough or scary.

They looked foolish. Their garments were harmless. They were costumes.

This was not about their clothing, though.

On their backs, they carried real rifles.

On their bellies, they strapped homemade bombs.

In their hands, a hunting knife (West) and machete (Mark).

At first, people thought it was a stupid prank or possibly even some dazzlingly inappropriate skit the cheerleading squad had cooked up about going to war against our rivals or something stupid like that. But it didn't add up. From the accounts of those who survived, I learned that "something felt off."

The bus idled and gave off that fumey public bathroom-like scent as it sat in the parking lot. It was like any other bus. Up they walked. Up the steps and onto the bus. "We're taking over," Mark said. Then he held his pointer finger up to his lip in a move he must have practiced and said, "Correction. We've taken over." Everyone knew who these two jokers were and expected nothing less than stupidity from them, and yet the glassiness of their eyes was frightening. They were having too much fun and one thing everyone knew about these losers is that they never had fun. Someone'd even nicknamed them Doom and Gloom. Still, it seemed weird that they'd come onto the bus armed. Some people even laughed nervously and shared pictures of them. Those pictures would circulate later on television and in newspapers around the world. Mark is smiling in them. Hamming it up for the camera. West, on the other hand, looks terrified. I cling to his terror. I want to tell anyone who'll listen, which is exactly no one: "See? He didn't really want to do it. He was brainwashed. He was blackmailed. He was scared." But I keep my mouth shut because he did do it. No matter what. My brother did it.

Next they took the keys from the bus driver and told everyone to shut the eff up and not move and things got serious and quiet. The balloon was dropped. Some of the girls started to cry. The coach was heard whispering a prayer. *Heavenly Father, protect us.*

Aaron Fowler, the point guard, panicked and tried to rush them. People later called him a hero, and I do believe he was one. He did what many people think they'd do, but probably wouldn't. What he did was try. He tried to make it stop.

Mark whacked him across the neck with a machete and then chopped at him on his arms and shoulders as everyone watched.

Then, at Mark's direction, West stabbed him in the stomach.

After that, Mark and West started slashing their way through the people sitting in the front seats using the knife and the machete. When someone tried to open the emergency exit in the back of the bus, they pulled forward their rifles and started shooting. People hid beneath seats and under fallen bodies, as Mark and West pushed their way to the back of the bus. Their aim was to get to the players back there. The big, popular guys who'd allegedly teased and bullied them through high school, calling them faggots and retards and dipshits. Tripping them. Knocking their books out of their arms.

When he finally made it to the last seats, Mark raised his hands to the sky and shrieked, "Vengeance is mine." Then he detonated a homemade bomb that was supposed to be powerful enough to blow up the entire bus. Instead, it killed only him, tearing out his stomach. The shrapnel from the bomb maimed those nearest to him. West didn't die on the bus. We're unsure whether he tried his bomb or not. My guess is that he chickened out. Realized too late how wrong it all was and ran. He discarded his costume and rifle in a garbage can near the bus ramp and ran home because there was nowhere else for him to go. West freed himself from the carnage he'd inflicted on other human beings while the ones who survived stayed behind and bravely tried to administer to the wounded while they waited for help to arrive.

Six people were dead and twelve people wounded, many of them still in critical condition. I'm supposed to feel something for these people, and I do. Especially when I think of them individually. But taken as a group I'm overwhelmed by them. Many have scars deep beneath the skin that will never heal. When I see the individual faces on the news, from school pictures, from family photo albums, I feel like I am each of them. Like it could've been me. I wonder how many people look at me and wonder if their own brother is capable of such a thing.

Allegedly, the motive for the mass murder was revenge against the bullies, and revenge against the country that had failed them by raising the bullies, but it was mostly, according to Mark's journal, an unquenchable desire to find out what it felt like to kill another person. He wrote that he thought it would feel "amazing" to kill someone.

As for my brother, I don't know his motive. When he came home that night, he was beyond words. Out of reach.

Now here's the part that I know for sure. The part that involved me. That night, I was home like every other night, wishing that I was anywhere else but home with my mother and Archie.

I was on my bed, back up against the wall, my KEEP OUT sign firmly in place, door locked, chair up against the knob in case the lock didn't work, headphones on, unaware. I thought my mother and Archie were out there, drinking, laughing at something stupid, while they planned their pathetic wedding, which was still a few months away. I didn't want to hear them. I assumed that later they'd be in their bedroom next to mine, doing stuff to each other that I definitely did not want to hear through the thin walls. Hearing your mother and her boyfriend hooking up once is enough to scar you for life, believe me.

So when West got home, I had no idea he was there. He was supposed to be out all night. The noise I heard? Like I said, I thought it was them in their bedroom. Gross. I heard banging and felt thumps against the wall and thought that maybe they were fighting. I'd given up trying to stop them. Whenever I'd stepped in before my mother had pushed me back out of the way. I wondered if she wanted it to happen, like a punishment she expected. Maybe she thought she deserved it. I would've felt sorry for her if I didn't hate her for bringing Archie and all of the Archie-types before him into our lives. I just wanted her. I wanted it to be the three of us. We were supposed to stick together and not let anyone or anything come between us, but I was the only one who still held onto that idea. West was always off with Mark. Mom was with Archie. I was alone.

I turned up my music. I let it bang into my ears and through my blood. Punish. Punish. Punish me. More banging. A thump against my door. Another thump. I sat up. Someone was trying to break into my room. The door cracked, splintered. I pulled my headphones off my ears and heard West screaming at me, "Let me in, Laney. I need to get in." There were other voices, too, yelling at West. Telling him to put his hands up. To drop his weapon. They asked again. And then they shot him.

And that is how my brother died. Outside my door, screaming to get in so that he might kill me. His body slumped on my threshold, in his hands a hunting knife covered in my mother's blood.

I was made to lie face down on the sticky kitchen floor with my hands behind my head while the police searched the ratty ranch-style house we rented. When the leader gave the all clear, they let me stand up. Someone handed me a damp paper towel so that I could wipe some dirt off my face. Really, at that point I didn't care what was on my face. I just wanted to know what was going on. I kept asking the question—what's going on? —but no one seemed to hear me. If they did, they were ignoring me.

Then Archie returned from the package store with a fresh bottle of vodka to find the house surrounded by cop cars. He came into the kitchen then, finally, once he'd persuaded them he lived there. "Your dad's here," one of the police said to me.

He's not my dad, I thought to say, but didn't or couldn't. Instead, I asked, "Where's Alice?" No one answered me.

They took Archie aside and filled him in, while someone asked me if I wanted tea. I stared at her and wondered what would make her think we had tea in our house, or a kettle, for that matter. I said, "Where's my mom?" That's when Archie came over, crying, and hugged me. "She's gone, Laney," he said. "Your mother's gone."

"Where?" I said, pushing him off of me. "Where is she?"

"She's passed away," Archie said, holding me at arm's length. Bruising my face with his wasted eyes. "West killed…"

"Shut up," I said. "Get off me." I pushed away from him and tried to run from the kitchen but hands and arms reached out and stopped me. Bodies covered my body and held me back. I'd never been touched by so many people at once, and yet I'd never felt more alone. Everyone I'd ever loved was dead.

They questioned me later to find out how much I knew. I knew what West had done, and I already knew that he was dead. I knew that he'd killed our mother. But I didn't know why.

That was three days ago. Now a ruckus at the smaller of Mrs. Coughlin's bird feeders demanded our attention. It was the feeder she typically loaded up with expensive black sunflower seeds. Two gray squirrels were fighting over the perch. Mrs. Coughlin aimed, shot. Ping! She missed, but the squirrels tore off anyway. "Gotcha," she said, from her floral cushion, but it never did show them. Those squirrels would always be back.

The wicker seat creaked as she shifted her weight to stand. "Until tomorrow, Laney Kates," she said. My eyes were back on the bird feeders as I heard the back door shut behind her. Soon the squirrels were back plucking at the seed with their ratty claws. I caught a flash out of the corner of my eye, something red streaking by. I turned quickly, but missed it. Was it him?

Everywhere I looked, I saw West. Or thought I saw him.

I wished I had a gun.

But West was dead and all I felt about him being dead was relief. About my mother, my thoughts were pushing against my skin. I wanted to have not had my headphones on that night and to have heard him attacking her. I might have been able to save her. I pictured myself with super-human strength, fighting against West, taking his knife and turning it on him. Maybe I could've saved her. I desperately wanted her back.

I was angry, too, that the two of them went off together and left me here to clean up the mess.

I wore my brother's crime like a second skin. It constricted me, tight like a snake's skin I feared I'd never shed. That was who I'd become: The sister of a murderer. Not even being the daughter of the murdered could erase it. From that point on, my identity belonged to no one but West.

Two

I was kept away from the house—the crime scene—for a day and a half. A female police officer brought me to a hospital where I was poked and prodded and spoken to as though I were an absolute idiot. I did not cry. I barely spoke. My brain felt black and when I told them that the doctor said I was in shock. A nurse patted my arm. They put me in a private room, gave me a bed and some medicine to help me sleep. A police officer guarded my door. Later, I learned that I was at the same hospital as many of the victims. Maybe their families passed by my door. Maybe they were on the opposite wall. I'll never know for sure. All I do know is that we were once again connected by the horrible crime my brother committed.

A woman named Marta stayed with me. She told me she worked for the Department of Children and Families and was my case worker. They hadn't let me see her, my mother, and whenever I brought her up, Marta changed the subject. When I asked her why she was there, she told me she was there to help me. She was supposed to be nice, but behind her smile, I saw her weariness. I saw that she didn't really care that much. I saw that she was over it and maybe a little scared of me, as if I were just like my brother.

Marta's hair was the same color as my mother's: reddish blonde. Strawberry. My mother. But Marta was older than my mother, softer. Where my mother had been rusty edges covered in thin skin, Marta was curves covered over in layers of tissue.

Marta, mother. I was beginning to confuse the two. I wondered if my mother had ever really existed. Maybe she'd just been a dream. Maybe West was a dream, too. Or a nightmare. I wanted to sleep and wake up and know that nothing bad had happened. Ever. My sleep was deep and impenetrable.

When I woke in the late morning, I saw that Marta was still sitting in the chair beside my bed. Maybe she'd gone home and come back. I wasn't sure. Her clothes seemed the same, but they might have been different. As it was, they were plain and simple—jeans and a t-shirt. A cardigan. On her feet, she wore clogs like the nurses wore. Her face was the same as it had been. That much I remembered.

"How're you feeling?" she asked. She asked me that often. I think she was really supposed to want to know how I was feeling, but her voice was slippery and so I couldn't grab onto it.

"I'm okay," I said, and winced. My mother's face and then West's. They were pinched into my brain. I squeezed my eyes shut and pushed them away. "I want to go home," I said, but I didn't really mean it.

"Tomorrow," Marta said. "You can go home with your dad tomorrow."

"My father's dead," I reminded her. I was sure she and I had discussed that in the frantic hours after transportation and hospital intake. "Archie's nobody." I felt both good and bad saying that because, while he was nobody, he was all I had right then.

"They were getting married, right?" Marta said. I nodded. They had told us at Christmas. It was meant to be a happy surprise for West and me, but neither of us reacted the way our mother hoped we would. West stormed off to his room, and I stayed on the couch and stared at the floor. "Aren't you going to congratulate us?" my mother said. She was happy, which made me even angrier. "We'll be like a real family," she said.

"We'll never be a real family," I said, which made her cry. I was pleased to make her cry, though I felt a slight twinge in my heart for doing so.

"Did you know that he and your mother had filed paperwork so that he could adopt you?" Marta asked. "The were in the final process of approval."

My breath blocked behind my teeth.

"He's agreed to watch you until we can find a blood relation." she said. There weren't many of those. So I had nothing. I belonged nowhere. I felt my body floating away from all that it had ever been connected to. It didn't matter if they sent me home with Archie. Nothing mattered.

"It's just for now," Marta said, easing me into the idea. "We're still making arrangements for you."

"You make arrangements for a funeral," I said. Marta frowned. Her frown did not stay in place for long, as my mother's had. Soon her mouth shifted back to its watery smile.

"We'll figure something out," she said, reaching over and giving my hand a squeeze. Her hands were so cold. Winter hands. The room was covering over with ice. I felt it in my own blood.

As promised, Marta brought me home the next day. "Remember," she said on the way there, "it's only temporary." This was the one truth in my life: everything was temporary, except for pain. But even pain could be erased.

We pulled into the driveway. Archie's car was already there, the trunk open and filled with hastily packed boxes. Yellow crime scene tape fluttered around the railing of the front stoop. We entered the scene. Outside what used to be my door, rust colored stains—blood, I soon realized—were circled on the carpet. Archie was in the kitchen, shuffling through the junk drawer.

"Mr. Mckenzie, I've brought Laney home," Marta said as we entered the room. She kept one arm around my shoulder, as though hugging me, but I felt in her muscles that she wanted to push me forward and be done with me. Archie turned and tilted his head like a puzzled dog.

"Hi, Laney," he said, frowning in a sad way.

"You've been packing," I said. Archie nodded.

"I'd better get going," Marta said, as if anyone was waiting on her back wherever she was going. The reality was she simply wanted away from this house of horrors, but not as much as I did, now that I was back in it.

"Please don't go," I said, reaching for her cold hand. I couldn't stand the thought of her leaving me yet.

"You're okay here," Marta said, rubbing my back. "I'll be back soon."

"When?" Tears came to my eyes, but quickly retreated. I had not yet cried, but Marta was leaving me. She could not leave me.

"I'll call you later," she said, "and I'll come back tomorrow morning to check on you." It would be a whole day away from her. No.

Next she was hugging me and I was clinging to her and then Archie was there pulling me away from her and Marta was leaving. I heard someone screaming. It was me. I was screaming.

"Come back. Come back. Come back."

After Marta left me, Archie and I entered the time of waiting. Archie was waiting to leave, to run as far away from this house and this town as fast as he could. The authorities were waiting for word from my relatives—some distant cousins of my mother, my grandmother, someone else and someone else. Someone to take me in. I was waiting for what would happen next. I was waiting to not feel horrible and sick and ashamed. I was waiting to find out who I would become. I was waiting for more sleep to give me relief from my itchy brain, which never stopped flashing at me. Images. Horrors.

Let's talk about who I became in the time of waiting.

I was the girl with the psycho brother who killed innocent people. I was that geeky, tall girl, the one you saw on television turning away from the camera, covering her face with her long hair. I was the girl who should've done something to stop her brother. I was the girl who was still alive when so many others were dead.

People in town wanted me dead. I knew that. I'd seen what they wrote online when newspapers published stories about the incident. I'd seen what they said on the news. People said things like, "We should hunt down their families and kill them," and "Why didn't their families do anything to stop them? Where were their parents? Didn't anyone suspect anything?"

The year before in school, some technology expert came in to talk to us. He worked for a police task force or something like that. He warned many times about the evils of the Internet. Warned us about how everything we said and did online became a permanent record of who we were and who we would be seen as. 90% of the people in the auditorium completely tuned him out, including me. But now as I read the many accounts of the incident online and read the comments that people left, most of which suggested that we, the remaining family, be dealt the same hand that the victims had been dealt, I started to wonder if maybe I should have listened to the expert. Maybe we all should have. But still, I understood that those people leaving comments were only looking for some relief, that they needed a scapegoat. I couldn't blame them. I might've done the same thing if the shoe was on the other foot, which it sort of was. Wasn't I a victim, too?

I'd lost my mother, after all. I wanted revenge along with them. But there was no target for my revenge. It was not enough for any of us that West and Mark were dead. We wanted them to pay even more dearly for their crime. Revenge was mostly what I thought about in the time of waiting.

The time of waiting seemed to last forever.

During the days, I took to the woods, the only place I could breathe. I felt the presence of West everywhere else. He seemed enormous then, even though he'd always been small. Thin body, thin face, large hands and feet. Alice, our mother, said he'd grow into his body the way our father apparently had, but I guess now we'll never know. When he was younger people picked on West for being small and for having crappy haircuts. Later, when we moved to this town, they called him names for wearing black nail polish. Then he met Mark and had an actual friend for the first time. West even cleaned up a bit, dressed down his look to be closer to Mark's more conservative appearance of polo shirts and jeans. Mark's family was different from ours. They went to church and had money. People said they were a "good" family. Mark had advantages. He had an older brother in college, pre-med. His parents had good jobs. Mark had his own car. At first, I wasn't really sure why he chose West as his friend. It seemed to me that with all of those things going for him, he could've been friends with anyone.

But once you knew Mark, you started to understand that he was not like everyone else. Mark stood outside of life. He mumbled. He had a scary laugh—high pitched and out of control. Mostly it was that his eyes seemed like the eyes of somebody who was already dead or wanted to be. The two of them called themselves INsane Killahs. They were obsessed with terrorists, foreign and domestic—Al-Qaeda, The Boston Bombers, the Unabomber guy, and even Timothy McVeigh, who blew up that government building in Oklahoma. They were also obsessed with all of the many kids who murdered people in schools across the country. Mark was particularly obsessed with two kids at Colombine, Dylan Klebold and Eric Harris. But he wanted even more notoriety. Mark wrote in his journal, "We are just like Eric and Dylan but we will be bigger than they ever were. We will be everywhere. The world will know who I am and the world will shake with fear. I AM JUDGMENT and only GOD can judge ME now and I am GOD."

Even though Mark wrote all of this stuff about God, what they did was not about God or religion or political beliefs. It was about two messed up kids who had no idea what to do with their anger. It was about the screwed up families who had spawned such monsters. It was about us. It was about Mark's parents and brother. It was about the survivors related to the monsters.

It was about me and all of the other people who didn't "understand" them. Understand what, though? I was left out at school, too. I was ignored and looked down upon, but I never would've hurt anyone over it. I just wanted to be left alone.

From my vantage point in the woods, up a rise, crouched behind an old stone wall, I could see our yard without being seen. I was on watch. I could see Mrs. Coughlin's yard, too. Reporters had been knocking on her door just as they had ours, except she answered the door with her BB gun in hand, whereas we kept our door closed and locked.

All winter long, birds and squirrels fought for the food she put out. There was always one who did not fight, but waited—the hawk. It was an easy meal for him if he caught one of the smaller birds. I liked to stand on our side of the fence and watch for him with my binoculars. Sometimes I made a noise if I saw his shadow on the ground—I was benevolent and alerted the birds and squirrels. Other times, I saw him and watched and waited. Often, I didn't notice him at all until he'd made his move. Mostly he missed out, but every once in a while he caught something—a wee sparrow, a plump chickadee. It used to make me sad, but then I realized that nature was just doing its thing.

That sort of killing the hawk did—the kind you do for food—is natural. Some animals kill to be the boss within their herd or to protect some territory they believe they own. Some kill out of fear. But most of them only kill for food. Otherwise, why waste the energy?

Killing for fun is not natural. It's not part of what God or

Charles Darwin intended. I would've told West all of this if he'd asked me. I would've said, "Don't be stupid."

But he was stupid and he wouldn't have listened to me anyway.

The woods were a quiet place to most people, but I heard all of the small noises. The rustle of squirrels in the dry leaves searching for nuts. I listened for the snow from the night before slithering to the ground from the branches of the swamp maples. Not so far off I could hear the ease and creak of the ice on the river, winding through the salt marsh.

I walked down to the river and watched the water slink by. Out across the marsh on that winter day, the golden grass shivered beneath a boldly blue sky. The wind picked up, pushing in snow clouds from the north and blowing frigid air up beneath my thin jacket, but still I wanted to be out there for just a while longer, breathing in and breathing out.

The breathing helped to cover over the remembering and thinking. My brain wouldn't stop if I didn't work hard to make it stop.

I remembered. I remembered that last week of school. The last normal week before everything fell apart. All week long there had been pep rallies, announcements. During last period on that Friday, most of the teachers let us sit around and talk. Everyone was too amped up to pay attention to social studies or physics or even sexual reproduction in health class.

West and Mark were probably excited, too, but for a different reason. They say some people experience a sense of euphoria before they commit suicide, which is essentially what they were doing. There is something about finally being free from your burdens. Maybe you also feel released from acting within the confines of society, letting go of the strong will to live. They both must've wanted to die.

I don't know. I want to live. I never want to die.

Mark's parents confirmed that the two boys met up at Mark's

house earlier that night. Mark's mother offered them dinner, but they said they'd already eaten. Food was irrelevant to them at that point. They were there to arm themselves—West had the hunting knife that Archie had won in a poker game and Mark had a machete he'd bought online. They had the rifles and bullets from Mark's dad's gun safe. They'd planned on using the guns and bombs all along, but also there was something about wanting to really feel what it was like to kill up close, to know the feeling of blade through flesh.

I have to stop there. I really have to stop there.

The memorial service for the dead was on the second night of the time of waiting. No bodies were present. It was a group thing. Separate funerals would be held later and privately. This was for the public, the town. It was for all who grieved those murdered.

The moon shone through my window on the night of the memorial service. My mother always told me never to look at a full moon through a window. Bad luck, she said. My luck could not have gotten any worse and so I openly stared at the moon.

What did you see, Moon? Did you witness these crimes? Will you forgive me, Moon?

The moon was silent, deathless. The moon, the moon. My mother used to read us *Goodnight, Moon* when we were small. I remembered her voice becoming quieter and quieter as she read until she ended with a whisper. I wanted to find that book then and bring it to her. I wanted to crawl into her lap and suck my thumb and have her read it to me. I wanted. I wanted.

The moon, cottoned over by clouds, shone like a thumbprint that night when all of those people were in the school auditorium, mourning the dead, praying for retribution. I wanted to give them something. I imagined that there were prayers and songs. I imagined that family members and friends stood at the microphone and testified to the greatness of their dead and the vastness of their grief at having lost them too soon at the hands of such monsters. The word *senseless* would be used a lot. There would be anger, but it would simmer quietly underneath the skin.

What could I have said for West, were I called upon? That he was not the brother I once knew. That he had changed. I could've said that I was scared of him, too. Because I was scared of him. He was the reason why I kept my door locked.

I looked for West in the moon fully expecting to see his face, but I did not see him there. He was not in the kitchen cabinets, either. Not under my bed. Not in the woods or the wind.

The moon shone on.

What was the moon like the night of the murdering? Can I remember the moon that night? Was it not just black out there in the yard? Did owls not swoop through the open space looking for a tree branch, or a mouse? I could do some research to find out about the moon that night, but research is not memory. It only aids memory. Glosses over the fine details of experience, bubble wrapping emotions so that they do not break.

The moon. The moon is not equal access. The moon does not belong to everyone.

The incarcerated will not see the moon from their jail cells. Don't have a romantic notion such as that—that jail is all windows and bars and moonlight glistening through.

Think cement. Think fluorescence. West should have been in jail, dreaming of the moon.

But the moon was dead to West.

As it should be.

If I could, I would push the moon away from myself forever. I do not deserve the moon.

•

On the third night of waiting, Archie and I sat in front of the television watching the news. Archie didn't really watch the TV, though. He stared at me and when I looked at him, that same sad smile that only made me angry. He grossed me out so much. His clothes were dirty. His fingernails were black with filth from working on his car. I don't know. Maybe I'm making him worse than he was. Memory is funny that way. Maybe my memory is colored by how much I hated him because my mother was dead and he was still alive. If he hadn't gone out for cigarettes and vodka, maybe things would've been different. It might've been him who was dead or he might've stopped West. He might've been a hero, but he wasn't. He might've been my father, but he wasn't that, either.

Basically, his presence was annoying and stupid. He was not a dad to West and me and adopting us wouldn't have changed that. He was not a friend. He was more like some useless project Alice had taken on. The more messed up and immature the guy was, the more appealing she found him.

I went to my room, pushed the crooked, busted door as shut as it would go. I went online in search of West. I found his videos. He and Mark doing stupid tricks on their bikes and skateboards. He and Mark tormenting ducks at the village green. He and Mark laughing and laughing and laughing. The more violent and inflammatory of the videos—those with guns and knives and threats—had already been removed. But there was one video of West alone in his bedroom that remained. "No one will ever watch this," he said. But I did. His voice was how I remembered it and it was almost as though he were still alive. I reached a finger out to touch him on the dusty screen. "No one cares," he said, He turned off the camera and disappeared into the black.

I had given up counting the long days and even longer nights. I took to the woods even though Archie had hung signs up all over the trees surrounding our yard: "Keep Out" and "Private Property." This was to keep away the press and the psychos, but also to keep us in. I wanted to be kept out. I very much wanted that—to be on the other side of the signs with the regular people who were not us.

Already Archie had changed our telephone number because we'd received death threats. "You will pay for what your kid did," one of them said. "Don't you have a daughter?" asked another.

On the morning we woke up to find that someone had spilled red paint on our driveway and written "DIE" in front of our house, Archie freaked out. "Marta called," he said, pacing the kitchen, smoking. It pained me to hear her name. She had come only once since dropping me off. She called, daily at first, then once every other day or so. I yearned for her to be near me, blanking me out with her watery eyes. "They've gotten in touch with the old lady," Archie said, and I knew they were thinking of sending me away, up north. To her. Way up in the cold and dark where all of my family was born, but where none of us had wished to return. My mother rarely spoke of that place, and when she did it was with the tinge of a threat and danger. She threatened to send West and me up there many times before and it always worked to get us back on track. Or it always worked to get me back on track, anyway.

We'd lived up there once but my memories were vague. When I tried to picture what it was like, I saw bright light on white snow and dark green needles on tall trees. I heard a cold wind howling down from Canada. My memories were more tactile. I could feel myself wrapped in many blankets against the cold. I could feel the tip of my nose as it started to freeze.

Up north.

They would send me up north where no one I knew lived and where no one knew me and this would magically make me safe. Way up where my mother left with us all those years ago.

Staying with Archie didn't seem so bad after all. "Can't I stay with you?" I asked him.

"Not an option," Archie said. He rubbed the palms of his hands together over and over. I could tell he was counting the seconds until he could ditch me and leave.

"But you were going to adopt us," I said, playing my trump card.

Archie stopped pacing. "So you know about that, huh?"

"Marta told me."

"It was the only way your mother would agree to marry me," he said. "She wanted you kids to have a father figure. Especially West."

"Whatever," I said.

Archie grabbed my shoulders. "Look at me, Laney," he said. I would not look at him. "Okay, then don't look at me, but hear me: I loved Alice. I would've done anything for her."

"Except save her life." I pulled away. "It should've been you."

"I wish that, too," he said. "It should've been me." We stood quietly for some seconds, and then he said, "There's a job waiting for me in Maine."

"Take me with you," I said. Anything seemed better than going back where they were sending me.

"Everyone just wants you to be safe," he said, pressing his palms down against the air as if to prove that he meant what he was saying. As if I ever had been safe. "It was what your mother would've wanted," Archie said. "What she would've chosen for you."

What a crock.

Her choices made me unsafe. She was the one who took us from there in the first place and moved us from state to state and from town to town until we ended up in this coastal town of Massachusetts. She was the one who chose crappy boyfriend after crappy boyfriend until she ended up with the crappiest boyfriend of all, Archie. She was the one who chose to take care of the men in her life over her kids—to listen to those men, to trust them. She was the one who chose to go out drinking most nights instead of staying home with her children.

"How would you know what she would've wanted?" I yelled at Archie as I stormed out of the room. Just like everyone else, he didn't want me. I didn't want him, either. He would be as alone as I would. There was some satisfaction in that. I wanted him to feel this pain.

That afternoon, the funeral director came to visit us at the crime scene instead of having us go to the funeral home. He wore sunglasses and a baseball cap. He'd dressed down in jeans. "I hope you understand," he said when he arrived. "The press and all…"

We understood. We more than understood.

As the next of kin, I decided to have my mother and brother cremated. The idea of caskets and funerals and burial plots was all too much. I would receive the ashes in a week or less. They were willing to make things go quickly to be done with us. Two cardboard boxes each filled with a plastic bag of ashes that had once been my family.

After the funeral guy left, Archie told me for certain that he couldn't take me with him. I was going north. That was it. "Marta is coming over later to work out the details," he said.

"I hate you," I said. I said it just like that, quietly, calmly, and then I left the room and him in it. But really it didn't matter if I stayed or went. My life was ruined, anyway. It had never been anything but ruined from the minute I was born.

My last hope was that Marta would keep me. I would ask her that. I would make her see that it would be good for us both. I would be the best daughter to her. I would love her and she would cherish me. It would be perfect.

The next time I saw Marta, I could hardly focus on what she was saying. Marta, my savior. "I'm going to drive you up there," she said. "Your grandmother is waiting for you. It took us a while to track her down." I stared at her, willing her to see the error of her ways. I belonged to her now. She would have to see that. My plan was to convince her in the car, when she couldn't get away from my voice. She would have to listen to me there.

On my last night of waiting, I lay in bed thinking of the victims, picturing each one face by face. Trying to remember if I'd ever heard all of their voices. What did it sound like when Rob Jeffries coughed? What perfume did Lisa Cliff wear? Was it flowery? Tangy? Did Mr. Cross walk with his shoulders up or down? I wanted to draw them all into one portrait. Get them all in place like a family. Then I wouldn't have to worry so much that they were alone and scared wherever they were.

My eyes sought the ceiling. Beyond the ceiling, the sky, the stars, the moon. Beyond the moon, the universe. I pictured them in a black, dreamless sleep. No stars. No air. A thick blanket of black.

I shut my eyes. Squeezed them tight and held my breath, trying to will myself to stop thinking of what happens to us after we die. I didn't want there to be nothing left of me. Or maybe I did want there to be nothing left. Maybe I didn't deserve anything more than nothing. But I wanted more.

Give me a sign, I thought. Give me a sign.

I must've fallen asleep then because later I woke up and the house was completely silent and still. Outside the moon had shifted and filtered in through the slats of my blinds. I had the sensation that something had woken me up. Someone was in the room with me. I almost called out West, but covered my mouth with my hand to stop his name. West would never be there again.

I heard a sound like an object moving through air and then a soft thud against the wall. Was it an animal? A bat? A bird? I covered my head with my blanket and listened. No sound.

I waited and counted to one hundred, two hundred, three. Nothing. I uncovered my head then and stuck my hand out to turn on my light. The room was just as it had been. No one was there but I felt as though I was not alone. The air shifted around me like a breeze. I turned my head in the direction of the noise, where something had struck the wall. There in the shadow was something brown and bright green. I got up from my bed and eased over to see what it was. Dirt and moss. But it wasn't physically there. I was seeing it as if through a hole in my current existence. It was overlaid on what was before me. I tried to touch it and felt nothing.

My brain went fuzzy for a while, like feedback on a television, a station coming in not quite clearly.

I thought I might be getting a headache, another migraine like I'd been having at night during the time of waiting when all of the images and memories crowded over me. Just before sleep each night with increasing intensity my head pounded with blood, pressure: a headache that no painkiller could reduce. On top of the pain flashed those unwanted images and impressions of what it had been like on that bus. I envisioned the people sitting in their seats excited for what promised to be a great game—the game of the season. I sat in a bus seat and watched as West and Mark walked down the aisle. I watched as West lifted his gun and put it to my temple. Worse, I watched as he raised his knife above his head, ready to plunge it into my chest and with the impact of the blade, the pressure in my head lessened and I slept. Mornings, I would wake and wonder if I was going crazy. I was like West. His brain had infected mine. I was sure people would be able to tell. Through the day, the visions would fade but at night the visions kept coming and I wondered when I'd be found out.

But this sensation was different than before. Stronger. The pressure pushed against my skull then and opened up like a bubble in my brain, and then it released like when ears pop at the top of a hill. Another vision, but stronger this time, more in focus.

It felt like it was really happening then and there.

The vision was like someone else's memory. The hands of the memory were not my hands, yet I could feel what they felt. The breath that came out of me huffed and labored in the work. I felt it as though it were my breath. I recognized the space. We were out back near where I had seen such bright moss earlier in the day. It was back beyond the yards, back near the stone wall. Back where West used to hang out and smoke cigarettes. The hands were scratching at the earth beneath the wall and once the hole was big enough, they put something wrapped in plastic into the hole. I could almost feel it. Hard beneath the plastic. A book. The voice that was not my voice said, "Are you coming?" Then the pressure pulsed and lifted and the memory faded away.

"Who are you?" I whispered to no one and felt the hair on the back of my neck rise as though a hand had passed over my skin. It took me only a few seconds to realize that the voice I had spoken within the vision was West's voice.

I sat in my bed and watched and waited for the first peep of sunrise before I dared leave my room and head out back. The wind picked up with the sun as I made my way out into the yard in the gray light. Late season oak leaves clattered from the trees and swirled around me. I carried a flashlight, a soupspoon for digging, and a dull steak knife in case I needed to defend myself.

I wondered if I would find West alive and laughing, telling me it had all been a big joke played on me. Maybe I had only imagined the sound and maybe the dirt and moss had come in on my shoes earlier in the day. Maybe it had all been a dream. It was possible. But I didn't want to explain anything away. I wanted a sign. I wanted some connection to what had happened and what was happening.

In my head, I carried a vision of the clod of earth and moss. I felt it was almost pulsating—a beating heart, drawing me forward. The wind pushed against my back. The branches cracked and shook above me. At the wall, I was disappointed at first. Nothing seemed out of place or disturbed, but as I walked back toward West's spot, I found a small collection of his used cigarette butts and a few empty beer cans and a spot where moss and dirt had been torn away. I pushed away the light snow cover. The moss in my head would have fit into that spot like a puzzle piece. My hand shook as I drew it away. I hadn't dared come out this far. It was West's domain and I knew not to get too close. Once, when I had gone into his room to borrow a pen without asking, he threatened to gut me with Archie's hunting knife.

I stared at the rock. I thought of the voice again from the previous night, *"Are you coming?"* The wind might've been blowing around me, but I was calm and quiet. There, beneath the rock, I saw a piece of clear plastic sticking out, like a kitchen storage bag. I took out the spoon and dug at the frozen dirt. It crumbled and gave way with surprising ease. I pulled the bag and out it came. Inside was a notebook. Written on the cover in thick black marker: THE BOOK OF WEST. Just then I heard our screen door creak open and Archie's voice calling out for me. I put the book back into the bag and stuffed it under my jacket. It was mine now. Someone or something had made sure that I knew it existed. Wherever I was going, it was going with me.

That afternoon I finished packing for my trip up north. Marta sat in the kitchen, talking to Archie, going over paperwork, thanking him for his patience and telling him how hard it had been to get in touch with my grandmother.

I stood outside of their view and listened.

"She doesn't have a phone," Marta explained. "I had to get in touch with the local police, who then put me in touch with the post office, who then put me in touch with some woman who relays messages to her." Archie murmured something that I didn't hear. "Right," Marta said. "No electricity. No running water. No cell service. But, apparently, she is able to survive like that. It's not for me, but who am I to judge? And who knows? It might do Laney good to live like that for a while, away from technology and the media. She'll be so far off the grid that none of these vultures will ever find her."

This was worse than I'd thought it would be. I knew the place was remote, but I didn't know that I would be completely cut off from the outside world. No electricity? There was no way I was going to live there. No. Way. If Marta left me behind, I would run so far from there that no one would ever find me. Not even Marta.

I remembered very little about my grandmother. All I knew for sure was that her house was on a bluff on the backside of a large lake in the Adirondack Mountains in New York State. A lone road led to her house, impassable in winter. Marta seemed to think it would be the perfect place for me to be safe, but I couldn't help feeling like crap about it. West had committed the crime, but I was the one being punished. I wanted to yell out to the world that I was innocent. I wanted to go to those reporters on the street and show them my two arms, unscarred, unfettered.

I leaned over the fence and waved to Mrs. Coughlin.

"I'm leaving soon," I said.

"Up to live with the old lady?"

"Yup," I said, "but no one is supposed to know where I'm going."

"I'm not no one," she said, turning her gray eyes to me. She'd been our babysitter when we moved in, even though our mother rarely paid her. She'd helped me get ready for bed. She'd helped West with his homework. She knew us as much as anyone did. In fact, sometimes I thought that maybe she was my only friend.

And I knew her. I knew she liked to sit in the cold and shoot at squirrels, and I knew that as much as she would pretend otherwise, she'd miss me. "You be good," she said tapping her fingernails. "Don't cause trouble."

"I won't," I said. It would be impossible to cause trouble in my exile. I wouldn't even be able to watch television. No computer. Nothing. Not even cell phone reception, not that I had anyone to call or text.

"I know you won't," Mrs. Coughlin said and then she got up and went inside. I thought she might even have been crying. I might've told her that I'd send her a letter, but I wasn't sure that I would. Once I was gone, I was gone. I'd learned that much already from all my leavings.

Out back I found my favorite tree—a silver birch. I stroked its bark. "You be good," I said to the tree. I felt like Lucy in Narnia talking to the trees, willing them awake so they might help fight the battle. If only they could've risen up then and saved me. Light filtered down through the crowding branches above, sparkling the snow into prisms and rainbows. I heard gulls in the distance. High tide. Soon I would be on a frozen, tideless lake way up in the Adirondack Mountains, hundreds of miles away from where I was right then in Massachusetts. I would miss the tide. I would miss the gulls. I would miss everything, even though nothing was left. "Don't cause trouble," I told the tree. Marta was waiting for me. It was time to go.

Archie wedged the last of his bags into the trunk and slammed it shut. "See ya, kid," he said, as he got into his rusty car.

Meanwhile, there was a photographer out at the road taking my picture. I hung my head, covering my face in thick hair. I heard his camera click, click, click.

What no photographer's lens could capture was that something had happened that opened me up just a little bit, and cracked through my anguish. The vision had brought me West's book, and even though I was being exiled, it was up to me to keep going forward so that I could find out what would happen next.

Three

I was told to pack lightly. My books were left behind. I was told to use the local library. I was allowed to bring one suitcase and one backpack. "I'm sorry you can't bring more. It's policy," Marta said as she put my bags in her trunk.

We were leaving the crime scene. We were leaving the time of waiting. We were leaving my home, in the car, next to each other, ready to go. Before she even turned the key, I said to her, "Please don't send me there. I don't know her. She lives like a crazy person. I need...I need stability. I need you, Marta. Please keep me." It was more than I'd said to anyone in days. It was more than I'd ever even said to her. I had no idea what her life was like. Whether she even had a home. Or a family. She was a blank slate. For a second, I thought she might say yes, but what I mistook for possibility in her eyes was actually blankness.

"Everything's already been arranged, honey," she said. "Your grandmother is waiting." But I knew it was more than that. She didn't want me. No one did.

I slumped in the passenger seat of Marta's Honda Civic, my hood up over my head, ear buds squished in as far as they could go. I wasn't even playing music. I just wanted to be clear that I was not talking. I took a last look at the river as we drove over the bridge—water pushing out to sea, dragging everything in its way with it. I wondered if I would ever see the ocean again. I cracked the window and breathed in one final breath of salt air before we hit the highway. When we were younger, West and I plugged our noses at the salty, sulfury smell of the salt marsh, but our mother had always loved it. "If you ever move away from here," she said to us, "you'll miss that smell." I knew now that she'd been right about that and some other things and I was wrong about so much. I was wrong about Marta. She was not my mother and couldn't be.

I didn't want to live with her, anyway. First of all, she had many annoying habits, like sighing. Marta sighed frequently. I wasn't sure if she was irritated or bored or if this was just something she did. As much as I did not want to go away, living with that sighing would have driven me insane. As would the fact that she was a cuticle chewer, constantly gnawing away at her fingers. The skin on her hands was wrinkled, freckled, dry. She wasn't so very old, but her hands looked it. I didn't want to be old, staring down death.

"What's your favorite subject?" she asked. She was someone who couldn't handle being alone in thought.

"You mean, in conversation?"

"No," she laughed. "At school."

"Math," I lied.

"Play any sports?" She was getting desperate.

"No."

"How did your parents meet?" she asked. I shrugged. As if I'd know. I barely remembered my father. He'd been dead for much longer now than I'd ever known him.

As far as them as a couple, I didn't know much about Alice and my father. I knew they met when they were young. I think they got married when they were eighteen. They did this against my grandmother's wishes, because Alice was pregnant with West. I knew my father's name was Ben and that he was my dad, but I didn't remember much about him—big hands holding me up to the light, tossing me in the air. A shadow of his laughter. Sunlight, dark skies. He was there somewhere behind my memories. The most important and factual thing I knew was that he was dead, but I didn't know why or how he'd died. Natural causes, was all Alice would say when I asked her, though I sensed there was more to it than that.

Marta reached down and snatched up her diet soda for a sip. Out of the corner of my eye, I watched her to see if she would say anything else, but she finally allowed silence to fill the space between us. I stared out and down, watching the road pass. Listening to the rhythmic thunk of the tires.

The pressure came on again. I closed my eyes. It'd never happened when I was in the presence of another person. I feared Marta would notice that something was going on with me. Ask me questions. I tried to still my breathing.

I was in another car driving on a hot summer day. I was holding someone's hand. My hand in another hand. Holding. Warm and I felt safe and excited. Well, no, not me. I didn't feel that way. The person felt that way but I was able to feel that way through her. The mind that was not my mind kept thinking, he likes me. He is holding my hand. And the feeling she had was overwhelming, not just of desire but also of feeling safe for maybe the first time ever. Surrounding me was a feeling I didn't recognize. Love, I guess.

She wanted to absorb him into her. I willed her to look up from the hands and to his face to see him. I kept thinking, look up. And when she finally did. There he was, alive and tanned and white-teethed and beautiful: My father. Then blackness.

When I broke free of the vision and opened my eyes, I looked over to Marta. She looked just the same. As though no time had passed. I wanted to say something to her about how much my mother had loved my father. I knew that now from the vision. I opened my mouth and then shut it again. I wasn't used to feeling anything for my mother but anger. Maybe there had been something else about her that I'd never realized. Maybe she'd once known a love unlike any I had ever known. I felt it, that love. I wanted Marta to know. Not just about my mother's love but about me. About my visions. I could trust her. I knew I could.

"I need to tell you something," I said.

"Of course," she said, glancing at me. "You can tell me anything, Laney. That's what I'm here for. I'm here to listen."

"I see things," I said. "I mean, I've been seeing things."

"What things?" she said. "Do you mean like spots? Are you dizzy?" She was not the best listener, really, preferring to fill in the dots with her own questions.

"No," I said. "I'm not dizzy or anything like that. I just see things. I mean, I have these…visions, and it's like I'm living in them. Like living in someone else's body."

"Like dreams?" she said. "Like dreaming? Like nightmares?"

"No. Well, yes. I mean, kind of like that, but more intense. I'm not asleep when it happens. I sort of black out and then it's like I'm actually living and feeling and breathing for this other person at some point in their past. It's happened with my mother."

I took a deep breath. "And it's happened with West."

Marta put on her emergency blinkers and pulled over onto the side. She turned to me. "Laney, you've been under a great deal of stress. Of course, you're going to have nightmares. It's normal. If it affects your sleep, I can get you a prescription. Just ask, okay? I promise they will fade away soon."

"No," I said, frustrated, near tears. "You don't understand. They're not nightmares. They're real." My hands were hard fists against my thighs. I wanted to lash out in frustration. I clenched my teeth.

Marta unhooked her seatbelt and took me in a strong hug. "You're strong," she said. "You'll be fine. You're alive and you're strong and you're going to be safe. You'll see. It will all be better when you're up north." She held me like that for a long time. I knew I would never trust her again.

I looked out the window and followed the road with my eyes

as we snaked through New Hampshire, through Vermont, until we hit the ferry that crossed over to New York. I said nothing more to Marta about the visions. She'd written them off as nightmares, but what if she thought I was just plain crazy and put me in an institution? Maybe I was crazy. Maybe I was.

She nudged me when the boat started up, crashing through chunks of ice that covered Lake Champlain. "Want some fresh air?" she asked.

"No thanks," I said and shrugged back into my hood. I did want to get out but I didn't want to give her the satisfaction of thinking I was warming to the idea of being up there. I wanted her to assume I was miserable, which I was, but also I was just a tiny bit relieved to be away from my old life. There was a chance I could be another person.

"Okay," she said and got out of the car. There weren't many other cars on the ferry with us. Marta was the only person outside in the freezing wind, looking as wasted and dried up as marsh grass in winter, bending against the gusts of wind. She held onto the rail at the front of the boat. I couldn't see her face, but by the tilt of her head, I knew she had lifted her eyes to the sky.

The boat lurched and Marta held on. It would have been funny if we crashed and the boat sank. There would have been no saving us from these frigid waters. Years later they would find me at the bottom of Lake Champlain, my body a skeleton. I looked at my hand, the bones beneath the skin.

My hands looked like my mother's hands, all long fingers and tapered nails. I couldn't remember the last time I had held my mother's hand. I used to all the time, in parking lots, at the movies. I wanted to reach for her and take her hand in mine. I never wanted to let go. I wanted to reach for Marta. For anyone. Please don't leave me, I would say. Please stay and hold my hand and keep me from drowning.

Marta turned as though she could hear my voice in her head.

Her eye caught mine and she lifted her fingers to wave. Another weary smile.

Off the ferry, we headed west and north. Before we could get to my grandmother's house we had to cross over a mountain. The weather turned dicey and spat a cruel mix of ice and snow at the windshield. Marta wore black woolen gloves and clutched the steering wheel. They were gloves like my mother had worn. I wondered if they were hers. I thought of all that I had left behind for the authorities to handle. Marta told me they'd put everything in storage. I'd have the chance to look it over before it was auctioned.

My mother didn't have much. Some clothes. Knickknacks. Photographs. My favorite photo was of the three of us on the beach. West and I were little. Our mother looked beautiful, standing behind us. The way she used to look before the years wore her down. Before we wore her down. It used to be great when we were small. Just the three of us. West, Alice, and me.

I remember when West and I stopped respecting her. I was ten and he was eleven. We were at a McDonald's. It was a weekday and our mother had lost her job as a waitress at Friendly's the day before. She kept us out of school because she didn't want to be alone. She had not yet met Archie. I remember feeling hopeful, that maybe this time we would end up somewhere great. This time she would find the perfect job and the perfect new apartment and we would be home.

She drank a coffee while West and I ate Happy Meals. "We'll figure something out, you guys," she said. "I heard that the 7-11 is hiring." She blew into her coffee and tried to take a sip, tested it with her tongue and put it back down.

"A convenience store?" West said. He pushed his food away.

"What?" our mother said. "It's a job."

"It's embarrassing," he said and put his head in his hands.

"Watch it, mister," she said pointing her finger at him, but she had no power behind her words. We could tell.

"Whatever, Alice," West said. He'd never called her anything but Mommy before. She sucked in her breath and held it for a moment before letting it out, and then she smiled and seemed to like it.

From then on she was Alice to both of us. I think she liked that she was one of the kids instead of some boring mom. I wished she knew how much we wanted her to be boring and old and a mom. It sucked to have a mother who wanted to be your best friend and who wanted to share clothes with you. She was wearing one of my hoodies the last time I saw her. Dress your age, I wanted to say to her. Put on a cardigan or something.

She must have died in that hoodie. Her blood would have soaked through it, coated it. I squeezed my eyes shut at the thought of it. I'd managed to not think of her dead. Her death. Push it away.

I took my ear buds out and sat up straight, tested the connection of my seatbelt. Here was my dilemma: I wanted to die, and yet I did not want to die. I wanted to live, and yet I did not want to live. There was everything. There was nothing.

We passed through a few small villages before the mountain— ramshackle and sad, the houses look deserted.

"Big hill," Marta said, nodding in the direction of the mountain up ahead. We were used to the flat land by the sea. This mountain we drove up wasn't so much big as it was steep. The car struggled and then lurched forward as Marta gave it more gas. We swerved a bit, but she stayed with it and we made it to the top. "I grew up in New Hampshire," she said. "I can handle this." She grew up in New Hampshire. That was the most I knew about Marta.

Then we were up. Up there we were in a cloud. It was like being inside my head—I could only see the edges of things, not where I was going.

As we started down the mountain, the cloud let up and the sky opened before us into a nearly perfect blue. More snow on the ground twinkled in the fading sunlight. Soon darkness would come. "The lake is frozen," Marta said. She told me my grandmother was on the other side of the lake. We'd have to cross the ice, as there was no passable road. I'd skated, but only on a pond or in a rink. I didn't believe I'd ever been on a lake in winter.

Alice wouldn't have been worried about the lake. She'd lived this life, which was odd to me, that she had this whole world before I even existed. A life in which I wasn't even a thought. She became strange to me when I thought of her walking across the ice with Ben—with my dad, Ben. Mysterious. An enigma.

A few years back, we were driving on the way back from picking up groceries when Alice told me it was my father's birthday. March 8. It had only ever been a normal day to me, March 8, but then knowing that it had meant something to him made it special to me. I said, "Did he love me?"

"Sure. Of course," she said. "He loved you as much as he could love anyone." Not quite the answer I wanted to hear.

"Did he love West? "

"Of course."

"What happened to him?" The logical question would have been how did he die, but that didn't seem right to me. I knew there was something missing in what I had always been told.

"He passed away," she said, blowing smoke from her ever-present cigarette out her nose, which she did when she was impatient.

"I know that but how? How did he die?"

"You know how," she said.

"No, I don't." She had been evasive about it from the first time we questioned her. I was old enough by then to remember things more clearly. West asked her where our daddy was and she said simply, "He's gone." As we got older, she told us he was dead, but nothing more about it, no matter how we pushed. I always had the feeling West might know more than I did, but I could not get it out of him, either.

"Natural causes," she said. I crossed my arms over my chest. "What?" I didn't look at her. "I don't know what else to tell you, Laney. I don't know what you want to hear."

The truth. How about we start with the truth?

Marta clutched the wheel. For a second, I felt connected to her again, like we were making this journey together. Marta was all I had now and I was scared that when she left me, I would be lost forever.

The sun was setting fast as we moved down a long, dirt drive.

We pulled up to a trailer, not a house. The lot opened to a view of the lake, flat and white, surrounded by mountains. An outdoor light came on as soon as the car stopped and a woman stepped out of the house dressed in jeans, a Carhartt jacket, work boots, and a baseball cap.

She waved, walked over, opened the passenger door, and examined me. I turned to look at Marta and gave her a quizzical look. "I'm Chellie. We're family," she said. "I'm your mother's second cousin." She stared into my face and said, "Wow. You look just like her." I'd never thought so. Alice was smaller. Paler, too. She seemed delicate and breakable, whereas I just seemed tough. I always thought that West looked more like her, because his face was pretty like hers—the kind of pretty you hold your breath over. Not like my face. I had a face you had to stare at a while to understand.

The woman held her hand out to me and I had nothing else to do but take hold of it. Her skin was rough and calloused, but warm. She pulled me up from my seat. Just as I was taller than Alice, I was taller than her, too. I folded my arms across my chest, pulling my shoulders in as I'd learned to do all these years, tucking in my height so that no one would notice it and say something stupid. "Come on," she said. She ran up the steps into her trailer as we followed.

It was warm inside, but confined. I felt the walls pushing against me, like I was inside someone's sooty lungs. I couldn't breathe. I reached out my hand and leaned against the wall, bending forward. "You okay?" Marta said. She was beside me, feigning concern.

"I'm fine," I said. "Just cramps." But it was air that I needed. "I've got some ibuprofen in the car," I said and went back out. I had some of my mother's old cigarettes stashed in my bag. I wasn't really a smoker. I'd tried it once or twice and didn't like it, but I had nothing to lose now. I dug one out and headed down through the crunching snow to the shoreline. I should've lit up right there in front of Marta because she clearly didn't care what I did, but I wanted the space anyway, and the quiet. Chellie's voice was too loud and her body too close, seeming to fill up the whole room. I wanted silence and clear, fresh air so that I could fill it with smoke.

Darkness moved quickly down the sky. At the edge of the mountains I made out a bit of light from the sun. I was wrapped in my parka, but still too cold to believe. To the west was my grandmother's bluff. And before me the lake, frozen over from softness. Hard and dark. Unreachable.

The pressure, now familiar and almost welcome to me, filled my head. My eyes were neither shut nor open, and I saw us walking across the lake in winter: *me, West, Alice. No, I didn't actually see us. I was there. I was as I was then and maybe I wasn't walking.*

Alice was carrying me. I knew that I was crying. "I don't want to leave," I said. "I want to go home. Bring me back. I don't want you. I want my daddy." My legs were kicking and kicking, but Alice held me tight and marched forward silently.

The vision faded, the pressure lifted, and the cold of the present came back to me. It was difficult to tell where the land ended and the ice began. I took a step forward and thought that I was on snow-covered ice, solid as anything, but if I went through right then, I was close enough to the shore that it wouldn't matter.

I finished my cigarette and headed back in. Marta and the

woman, Chellie, were sitting next to each other on a nubby plaid couch.

Marta looked at her watch to check the time. "Your grandmother will be waiting."

"I'll call Marshall and get him over here," Chellie said. While she was on the phone, Marta scrutinized me. I stared back at her. She closed her eyes and swallowed.

"We'll reassess your situation come summer," Marta said without opening her eyes.

"You said spring before," I said. She had said spring when we talked earlier, when she rejected me.

"Summer," Marta said. "It's only a few months from now. Until then, I'll check in on you, of course."

She was done with me. I was to be alone in this wilderness with no protection. I would wrap myself in blankets against the cold and lie in wait for summer, when we would reassess.

West floated above me in the room, hovered in the stuffy air. He was as he was when we were younger and he would pin me to the ground, his spit hanging threateningly above my face. I wanted to squirm away from him, but didn't know where I could go that he was not. He was in everything. He was everywhere.

"Marshall's on his way," Chellie said. "You ought to get bundled up and ready to go. We don't want to be late for your grandmother." Chellie made a scared face and pretended to chew on her nails. Then she smiled and lightly punched my arm as though we were buddies. I cringed. "Marshall's a good kid," she said.

Stupid. There is no such thing as a good kid. We're all bad. We all have bad thoughts and do bad things. Only adults think that kids are good. Only adults are stupid enough to believe that. We're all beyond help.

West hovered above me. He pinned me down and once again I was unable to break free.

Four

The whine of an engine echoed up the lakeshore. Chellie was up out of her chair and pulling on her gear. She handed me a hat, mittens. Outside, Marta helped me get my bags out of the car. The lights on his sled raced up the lake and stopped in front of Chellie's house.

"Go on down there. He's got a helmet for you," Chellie said. So much for introductions. Marta helped me strap my duffle onto my back. She carried the other bag. She spewed small talk as we walked down the path, saying it would be the best place for me and about how I would have stability. Family. I slipped a bit and caught myself on a branch limb. My sneakers were not made for ice-covered snow. Marta helped me steady myself.

"Well, I guess this is good-bye," Marta said. Panic filled my chest.

"Aren't you coming?" I asked.

Marta shook her head. "Chellie filled me in on all I need to know." She smiled at me. "You'll be safe there. I'll check in with you via Chellie. It's all good." She looked at her watch. "You better get going." She hugged me briefly, but I kept my arms tight to my side. "Here," she said, shoving a piece of paper into my pocket. "This is my address and phone number. Call anytime, day or night. Though I don't often answer, so you should know that. I don't like the phone…it makes me nervous." She was babbling.

"It's time to go," Chellie said.

"You're really going to leave me here?" I clung to Marta then. "Please don't leave me." I wanted to push her away and also hold onto her as tightly as I could.

Marta pushed back away and held me at arm's length and said, "You'll be fine." Then she nudged me in the direction of the idling sled. I was more alone than ever. If that was the way it was going to be, then fine. I would go, but I wouldn't stay there. As soon as I figured out a way, I'd be out of there and heading for someplace great. They'd see then. They'd be sorry thinking how they knew me back when and had pushed me away.

Marshall sat, unmoving on his sled, the engine idling. As I approached, he indicated a helmet on the seat behind him. I wanted to apologize for dragging him out on this cold night to get my lameness across the ice, but he seemed uninterested in speaking. He didn't lift the mask of his helmet, so I couldn't see his face. He could've been anyone. He could have been West, even though he was larger than West had been.

I lifted the helmet and put it on my head, strapped it beneath my chin. I felt like a stupid bobblehead in the rear window—my neck thin and weak, my head heavy and unwieldy. When I was ready, he flipped down the visor on my helmet and gave me the thumbs up. I climbed on. My legs wrapped around him. Had I not been wearing a helmet, he would've seen my cheeks flush with embarrassment. But Marshall was a stupid name, anyway. I put my hands lightly on his waist. The only male I ever remember willingly touching was West and that was only after being instructed to push in closer to him whenever we took a rare family photo. He pulled me in tighter, but I pulled back. Chellie and Marta stood on the shore and waved goodbye as we headed out onto the ice.

As Marshall sped up, I pulled in closer and tried not to be aware that I was clutching the body of this stranger. I focused on the ice. This was the ice I would be forced to travel should I want to make it to civilization. Once it thawed, then what? A boat? I had a lot to learn. I didn't know why my grandmother chose to live as she did—so far from comfort and warmth. I would've argued that life didn't need to be so difficult, but then I was only fifteen and, apparently, not smart enough to know what was best for me.

The light drained from the sky and we were left in a world of bluish white, lit up slightly by the sled's headlights. I felt good in the freezing air, a million, billion stars above us. I wanted to let out a whoop, but held Marshall tighter in my excitement. I forgot about everything: West, my mother, Marta, the visions. I felt the air pushing against me, the motor beneath us.

Finally, we were at the bluff, Marshall pulled up onto a small beach. My grandmother was waiting there with a lantern in her hand. She wore a long hooded parka covering her face. Alice didn't have any photos of her, so I wouldn't have known her even if I could've seen her face. She was as unfamiliar as anything else in that cold place. I could see that she was tall, like me. Unlike me, she stood straight and didn't stoop. Marshall turned off the engine and I got off, though Marshall held back, his helmet still on.

"Dinner?" my grandmother called out to him.

He opened the visor on his helmet finally and spoke. "Can't," he said. I turned at the sound of his deep voice. It was his eyes I noticed first—so dark that they rivaled the night. I felt myself cracking through the ice and into his eyes.

"Until Monday, then," she said. Marshall pulled down his visor and was gone.

"Are you hungry?" she asked me. I opened my mouth to speak, but nodded instead.

"Good," she said. She turned to go, assuming I would follow, which I did. My stomach constricted. I longed to turn and run, follow the retreating tracks of Marshall's sled. I longed to follow the light from out of the sky. I could've turned and scratched through the ice until I made a hole to fall into.

Those eyes. Like falling through the ice.

But then there was something to look forward to—she said he'd be back on Monday. Two days away. I could make it until then. Come Monday, I would see him again, and I would figure a way out of this place. I would make a plan. For then, I just needed to find my way out of the cold.

Vague snatches of memory led me up the path. I'd been here as a small child. While it was familiar in one sense, it was more like something I'd seen only on television. Something that I was remembering as my own even though those memories belonged to someone else. Another vision. I didn't get the feeling I belonged there, not fully. I was in the in between, the purgatory, of belonging.

My grandmother was inside the house well before I made it up the path. Lanterns warmly lighted the windows of her house. Smoke rose from the chimney. I stood on the porch willing myself to be brave and turn the handle. When I finally did, I saw my grandmother squatted at the fire, putting in more wood. With her coat off, I could see her hair was black like mine, unexpectedly long and glossy. She was dressed in a wool sweater and jeans. On her feet, she had switched from boots into fuzzy slippers. She looked comfortable and warm, like she belonged in the cozy setting. I dripped melting snow onto the floor in my damp hooded sweatshirt, thin parka, and worn sneakers. When she turned it was like I was looking at an older version of me: the same blue eyes, the same straight nose. I looked more like her than anyone else. Maybe that's what Chellie had meant with her comment—not that I looked just like my mother, but that I looked just like my grandmother. She was younger than I expected, but then I remembered that Alice and Ben were young when they had us.

"Well," she said, opening her arms, "As you know, I am your grandmother, but you will not call me grandmother. Instead, you will call me Meme, as I called my grandmother and she called her grandmother. It is our way."

I stood shivering by the open door. "And shut the door."

I entered a room filled with the peppery scent of cooking meat. My stomach growled.

"Warm up by the fire," she said. I pulled off my sodden sneakers and parka while she moved to the part of the room that was the kitchen to check on the stew.

I examined the room. Stuffed chairs, bookcases, a large fieldstone fireplace, a woodstove insert. There was no television anywhere. No electric lights. Lanterns lit the space and the room crackled with the sound of wood burning. It wasn't as dark and lonely as I would've thought such a place would be. It was more like the Mr. Tumnus the faun's house Lucy visits when she first travels to Narnia. Cozy. I found a seat by the fire where I warmed my stiff fingers. The gloves I had worn were a thin, synthetic material from a discount store. I would need better winter clothes to make it through the winter.

Soon, my grandmother—Meme—entered with a large pot. She put it on the table already laid out with bowls and spoons.

She beckoned me over to the table and I stood there dumbly. "Thanks," I said, but my voice came out like a croak. I cleared my throat and said it again. She finally looked at me.

"You're quite welcome, Elane," she said.

"Laney," I said. "That's what everyone calls me." Or used to, anyway. Now there was just us.

"Well," she said, nodding in my direction, "I'm not everyone. I am your Meme and I shall call you Elane." I shrugged.

I ate three bowls of stew and a half a loaf of bread before I was full. I didn't remember the last time I had a meal. As I finished my last bowl of stew, I looked up because I realized that my grandmother was staring at me. "My goodness," she said. "How am I going to keep you fed?"

I let my hair fall down to cover my face. Through the shawl of black, I saw her smiling. This glimmer, this gift, of affection would not crack me. She could try to break me down and break through, but I would not love her. In fact, I would never love anyone again.

After dinner, my grandmother showed me how the bathroom worked. Inside the bathroom, there was a cistern of water collected from rainwater throughout the year. She showed me how to use the toilet and the sink pump. We washed our faces with fragrant homemade soap and brushed our teeth in the chilly water and then she handed me a scratchy towel to dry off with. I saw a tub. "Where's the shower?" I asked.

"There's not one," she said. There was no shower. I repeat: no shower. Things were going to get ugly. "Just be happy you have an indoor toilet and not an outhouse." She was in front of the mirror, brushing her hair and smearing Vaseline on her face. "You'll take a bath once a week in winter," she said. "We'll heat up water for it on the stove. Other than that you'll have to make do." I screwed up my face at the thought of it. I was used to daily showers with plenty of hot water, provided our bills were paid and nothing had been shut off. We were certainly poor, but we were better off than this.

"You'll get used to it," she said. "It could be worse."

"How could it be worse?" I asked. "If I were dead?" She turned away. My mother would've told me to stop being so dramatic but I'd left my grandmother speechless. I didn't care if I did. I wouldn't get used to anything about this life. As soon as I figured out a plan, I'd leave for good.

We changed into our pajamas. She told me to keep socks on my feet and to wear an extra sweatshirt on top. Out in the main room, she led me up a ladder-like staircase into a loft. There were two large beds with a Chinese screen between them. "This is for you," she said, indicating the bed on the right. I climbed in and found that she had warmed the bed for me with hot water bottles and heated bricks wrapped in towels. I sank in and held my sloshy water bottle. In the dim light of her lantern I saw her move about, listened to the shuffle of her blankets, her sigh.

"Sleep well," she said.

My eyes adjusted to the dark. To my left was a large window looking out over the lake. Through the tree branches, I saw the sky illuminated by a nearly fully moon. The stars winked at me, each one a new friend. I'd never seen so many stars. I focused my eyes and tried to see beyond and beyond them. Somewhere out among them was West, hovering over me. Always watching and waiting. I couldn't quite make him out yet. He was still a smudge in the dark night, but I knew he'd show himself to me soon. He always did.

I woke to the smell of coffee and bacon. For the first time in days, I'd slept without visions. Maybe they were gone for good. Maybe time and space had made them fade away, and maybe I wasn't crazy. That could be the bright side to living in this place.

I stretched and shivered. The night before my grandmother had said to me, "A good trick for the cold mornings is to have your clothes underneath the pillow waiting for you. Your body heat will have warmed them up and then you can get dressed into them under the covers." I didn't want her giving me these tips because that meant I would be staying. Possibly forever.

"Breakfast," Meme called, and I got out of bed quickly and put as many clothes on as possible. Downstairs I warmed myself by the fire as Meme finished making the eggs.

Soon she called me to the table. I sat in the same seat I'd sat in the night before. Meme unfolded her napkin and placed it in her lap. Then she held up a hand. "I want to establish ground rules. If any of my rules are broken, I will consider sending you back to social services on the first bus out of town. At that point they can decide what to do with you. Am I understood?" I nodded in satisfaction knowing that there was a way out. All I had to do was break a rule and Marta would have to take me back.

"First," Meme said, "You will not go to school on a regular basis. You will go to school once every couple of weeks to pick up your assignments and then I will teach you here." Not that I wanted to go to some backwoods school anyway, but homeschooling? Seriously? Next she'd have me growing my hair down to my ankles and marrying my cousin.

"Second, you will help me around the house. I am not a maid or a cook or a washerwoman. I have serious work to complete each day on top of keeping the house running. You will be expected to do your fair share." Child labor. Awesome.

"Third, and finally, no boys. None." She did not elaborate. I looked down at my lap, embarrassed. I knew that she meant no sex and definitely no getting pregnant. I wasn't stupid. She wasn't interested in history repeating itself. Neither was I, frankly. Turns out she didn't have anything to worry about anyway because there weren't many boys who'd ever been interested in me anyway. Only the freaks, the outcasts, the untouchables. People like Mark. I was doomed to be alone. Just like her.

I picked at the placemat in front of me.

Meme picked up her knife and fork and ate. We were silent from then on.

I wondered if every meal would be so quiet. I was used to the television on and Alice and Archie either bickering or laughing together. I was used to West storming off to his room in a fury, slamming his door, cranking up his music so loud that you could hear it even though he had headphones on. I was used to so much more than this quiet room. We could hear the wind and the boards of the house creaking. We could hear logs snapping in the fire. I twisted my necklace around and around my finger and let it go. Twisted again and again and let go.

Alice had given it to me for my last birthday. It was a representation of my astrological sign, Scorpio. Whenever I was nervous, I rubbed the smooth metal between my fingers to calm myself. It had always worked until now. I couldn't shake the anxious feeling that I was going to do something wrong and make my grandmother angry. I wasn't used to rules. I would show her I could work hard, though. I would show her that before I left here. When I was gone, she'd think about how hard I'd worked and miss me.

After breakfast, I sat at the table and stared out the window at the blinding snow. "You can pick up the dishes and bring them to the kitchen," she said. I wasn't used to tidying up. We'd always eaten off paper plates. Pop Tarts for breakfast, that sort of thing. Meme heated water on the stove for the dishes. She gave me a pair of rubber gloves and showed me the soap. After I washed them, she had me wipe the dishes dry with a towel instead of leaving them to air-dry. She considered it more hygienic. She liked the counters and table wiped clean with a solution of vinegar and water. She composted scraps of vegetables and fruit and coffee grounds. Used paper and aluminum foil was folded and stacked in a cabinet to be used again. The amount of garbage she produced was minimal and burnable. Nothing was wasted.

She told me how once a week we would boil our clothes on the stove to wash them. "You are going to need to learn how to conserve," she said. "Water, heat, food. The necessities. Good lesson for a young person nowadays. In the spring and summer, there'll be more work with the garden," she said.

She didn't know I'd be long gone by then.

After we finished cleaning downstairs, she sent me upstairs to tidy. I searched the room for some place to plug in so I could charge up my phone until I remembered. Without power, there would be no outlets. Without outlets, there would be no electricity. Without electricity, there would be no contact with the outside world—not that I had anyone to contact, except maybe Marta.

I sat on the unmade bed. Then I fell back onto the pillow and pulled the covers up. My mother lived here like this. She must've wanted to go so far away, and yet she'd trapped herself. She'd allowed herself to love another and that had been her biggest mistake. I would not be so foolish. If my mother could live like this, so could I—for a while. This must've been her bed, I realized. I would not cry.

I woke up to the sun shining brightly through the window. I wasn't sure how much time had passed since breakfast. I heard the door shut and footsteps below. I got up to look out the window. Outside, Meme trudged across fresh snow, every once in a while her foot poking into the deep. I wished I had binoculars so that I could follow her as she walked. I thought she would stop soon, turn back, but she kept walking. I couldn't imagine where she was going. Maybe she would keep walking and leave me here. Maybe that was part of the plan. Maybe they got me out here so that I couldn't escape. She was leaving. She was leaving me.

I panicked that she was going to leave me there, and that I'd have to figure out how to survive on my own. I launched myself off the bed and got downstairs as quickly as possible. I shoved my feet into my sneakers and was out the door, slipping down the path.

It felt familiar to chase someone in this way. Scraps of memories pulsed over me. Running, chasing. My feet knew how to run. I'd been chasing others for most of my life—chasing my mother. If not with my body, then with my mind, always reaching forward for her even though it felt like she'd left me a long time ago. Like she'd never been there at all.

Mommy, Mommy, Mommy. Don't leave me. Don't leave me.

My mother's death was another leaving in a series of them. Her death was inevitable. I'd spent most of my childhood fearing that she would die. My biggest fear. Now that I was in the face of it, I didn't know how to feel anymore. Grief was almost a relief compared to a life of fearing she might die or leave and never return. She was gone. She was never coming back. Whenever that realization hit me, I felt my heart seize. A familiar panic.

Once she had a new job at night instead of during the day when we were at school. She left us with an old boyfriend. Not Archie. It seems to me that she wasn't even that serious about him. He was convenient. He was there. Been so long since I'd thought of him that I couldn't even remember his name. I only remembered that he liked to eat peanuts out of the shell. Crack, crack, crack. That was the sound of him and his peanuts. He would shell them and leave the shells on the floor and, when Alice wasn't around, order me and West to pick them up. She had to work, she told us, otherwise we would not eat. Still, I carried on every time she left for that job and it was West who tried to comfort me. "Don't worry," he'd say. "Mommy will be home soon." I knew it would be hours and hours before she would be home. Scary, lonely hours in which we waited. West knew this. He was just as scared as I was, but he made it his job back then to help me feel safe. But that West was gone now.

I slid down the path, not even feeling the cold. I found her footprints and ran with them, pushing through the snow. I bumped into Meme on her way up the path. She stopped me with her hands on my arms. "You're going to freeze in those clothes," Meme said as she pulled me up the path with her.

"Where were you going?" I asked.

"I was off feeding the rabbits, silly girl," she said.

"You have pets?" I'd never had a pet before. I longed for a dog, but rabbits would do.

"I'll show you how to clean their cages and care for them later."

Inside she sat me down by the fire and bundled blankets on top of me and I sat there until my teeth stopped chattering. I sat and watched the flames skipping and listened as Meme puttered around. In a while, she came into the room and handed me an old pair of her boots and told me to try them on. "These are old but still sturdy," she said. I pulled them onto my icy feet and immediately felt warmer. The boots fit perfectly. It was like they were mine already. They were lined with something soft and furry. "They fit?" she asked. I nodded. "Keep them," she said and then walked away muttering something about city kids.

I didn't want her stupid boots or anything else. I took them off and pushed them as far away from me as my foot could push them. My only hope now was to screw up so badly that Meme sent me away. It didn't even matter where I ended up. I just needed to be away from there more than ever because the fear that she might leave me was creeping in. I would not let her leave me. I would leave first this time.

I'd been staring at the fire for a long time when Meme offered me lunch. "I'm not hungry," I said. Meme rolled her eyes at me and sat herself down at the table anyway. She ate an enormous sandwich made on homemade bread. It looked good and I was hungry, but I would not eat. That would only please her. I knew the power food had over people. You can eat a lot of it and get fat and that gets people riled up or you can eat a little of it and get skinny and that makes people equally uncomfortable.

"Girls your age are very silly," she said. "I know because I was silly once, too. Listening to sad music, chasing after boys, not eating, being angry with my elders, thinking no one understood me. Boo hoo. It's all so insipid and uninspired." Meme stopped her diatribe to chew and swallow. She lifted a finger so I knew she would keep speaking. "Give me the girl who follows the rules and gets her work done and listens to her elders, and I will show you a girl who is a true trailblazer. Being good is radical nowadays, while being a rebel is expected." If she thought she was going to win me over with this bull, she was wrong. I could see right through her. She was trying to do reverse psychology on me or whatever, but she didn't know who she was messing with. I was an observer. I watched people for sport. I understood why they did what they did. I understood what they wanted. West was the only one who surprised me, and even that wasn't such a surprise.

Soon, she grew bored of me and cracked open a book to read as she ate. While she wasn't looking, I eyed her bookshelves. I missed my own books. The ones I'd always turned to for comfort at home. Books would be my only consolation there, but so much of what she had were books about nature. Books that I'd never heard of before.

"*Mammal Tracks & Sign*," she said, startling me. "Start there. You're going to want to know how to read the woods."

"I know the woods," I said. She snorted like she thought I had city girl written all over me. She didn't know me. Didn't know how many trees I could identify. Didn't know the birds I knew by song.

I looked at every other book and tried to force myself to find one that would be better than the one she wanted me to read, but my eyes kept coming back to the book she suggested. I sat down and put my hands under my thighs.

After a while she finished her lunch and tidied up after herself. Then she climbed into the loft. "It's time for my siesta," she said. When I heard her gently snoring, I got up from the chair and pulled *Mammal Tracks & Sign: A Guide to North American Species* by Mark Elbroch off the shelf. I brought it to the table and ate my lunch as I read. He talked about the experience of feeling like you're being watched: a feeling, he suggested, we'd all known at one time or another. I certainly had, Mark's eyes on me…or West's. It was like I was their prey and they were waiting for me to slip up. The more I read, the more I realized that the book was about learning to see in a different way. Maybe Meme was right. Maybe this was the book to read now. Find a way to learn about my place.

The rest of the afternoon passed quietly. Every time I felt I might cry for missing home, I focused on the book instead. When she came back down from her nap, Meme said nothing about my reading, but I noticed that she noticed and smiled smugly to herself. "I'm only reading it because I'm bored," I said before turning back to the book, but I'd found a way into the woods that I hadn't know existed. The book said that you don't just act as yourself as you track, but you become the animal, an idea which intrigued me. I'd found a way to see with my whole body and not just my eyes. It might be a way to unwrap the mysteries of the woods and maybe even the mysteries of my family. I would keep reading and learn about this other way of seeing. I would become the animal. I would become the woods.

Before dinner, Meme beckoned me up to the loft. In the corner of my section of the room there was a bulky steamer trunk. I had thought it was just a quaint decoration, but then I should've known better. I'd already learned that everything in Meme's house had a purpose. She pushed back the lid of the trunk. "You need more suitable clothing," she said. "Warmer clothes. Look through these things and see what fits. Otherwise, we'll have to take a trip into town." She stood up from where she had been kneeling and signaled me over. "This all belonged to your father and mother." I stood dumbly in front of the trunk, not sure how to begin. "I'll leave you to it," Meme said as she climbed down the ladder.

On top was an Irish fisherman's sweater—a real one that someone had knitted by hand. I'd always wanted one. I picked it up and unfolded it. Held it up to my face. It smelled of mothballs and the cedar lining of the trunk. Inside the neck was a label: "Ben." It had been my dad's. I held it up to me to see if it would fit. The sleeves would be long but otherwise it would do nicely. Beneath that were two pair of men's wool slacks. I stood and held them up to me. They would be too big around the waist but there was a belt

I could add some notches to and maybe Meme could sew them. I liked the idea of wearing my father's clothes. It was as though I was slipping into his skin. Maybe then I would understand why he had left us so soon. Not that you have a choice when you die. I had learned that much.

There were piles of thermal socks, which all would work for me as I could layer them one on top of the other. Turtlenecks. Silk long johns. Gloves that were too big. All of it seemed to be his and yet she'd said it was my mother's stuff, too. I pawed through what was left until I got to the bottom. There were two spiral notebooks, each with my mother's handwriting on the cover. There was also an old yearbook from Muskyville Central. I flicked through a couple of pages and put it back down for later.

I picked one of the notebooks and opened it. Schoolwork. Math. Boring. I didn't know why anyone would bother to keep the notebooks. I took them out and held them close to my chest. I lay down then on the floor, too tired to move. I closed my eyes and the pressure came back, so strong that it made me want to cry—not out of fear or pain, but out of frustration that the visions were still coming to me.

I was on a bed, in a room. It wasn't me. Of course, it wasn't me. The vision had me there. *The hands held a notebook like the one I'd found. They opened it up and started writing. I felt the pen in my hand and could feel and hear the words in my head but not clearly. They were coming too fast.*

I looked up from the paper and scanned the room. It was the same room where I'd slept but different. Fresher, happier. A white dresser held a lamp. A pink sweater was heaped on the floor. My legs lay across a worn quilt. They were bare and smooth, my feet still tan.

My feet. They were not my feet. My feet were cold and layered in socks in Meme's house. These feet, the feet I saw, were not mine but they were familiar to me. I could've sworn they were my mother's feet.

I tried to look back to the page of the book to see what the hand had written but the vision faded away again. No amount of trying could get it back.

When I came downstairs, Meme was sitting by the fire with a rabbit on her lap. "Oh," I said, delighted, "look at how cute it is." I ran over to her and reached my hand down to pet it. She shoo'd my hand away.

"Sit down by the fire," she said. "Watch and learn." She petted the rabbit on her lap until it relaxed, stretched its body out. It seemed in a trance. "You have to get them to be totally relaxed," she said. "In order to do that, you need to be relaxed yourself."

I did feel relaxed as I watched her stroking the rabbit. It was a lovely creature. Fluffy, its nose twitching. "Like I said earlier, we have more rabbits out in the shed in their cages. You'll help care for them."

"I didn't know you were going to have pets," I said, feeling hopeful for the first time since I'd arrived. "I want a dog."

"A dog is a lot of work," she said. "You've got to train them right."

"I think I could do it," I said. I was mesmerized by her hand on the rabbit's back. The bunny's eyes shut and as they did, Meme reached her hand around grasped its head and twisted fast. Snap. She had broken its neck.

"What?" I stood up. "Why did you do that? You killed it."

"These aren't pets, girl," she said. "The sooner you learn that, the less likely you are to become attached to them. This is our dinner. Come in the kitchen and I'll show you how to skin it."

I ran from the room and slammed the bathroom door shut behind me. I would not be eating that rabbit. Not now and not ever. She was crazy. She was a murderer. She was just like West. They had sent me from one crazy place to another.

"I'm not eating that," I yelled.

"Suit yourself," I heard her say through the door. "More for me."

The next day was a cage. I moved from room to room, constantly reaching for my phone before remembering that the battery had long since died. I needed to talk to someone. To let someone know that this woman was insane. That she'd killed a rabbit. A rabbit. Right in front of me. That was not normal. She was not normal. Clearly. I needed to call someone. Marta. She would understand. I had an imaginary conversation with her in my head.

"Marta, she killed a rabbit," I would say.

"I will come get you right away," Marta would say. "You will live with me and be my daughter. No one will ever scare you again."

One day, I would have this conversation with Marta. I knew I would. But this day was quiet and voiceless. This day was soundless except for the wind pushing around the walls and whistling in through the cracks around the door. This day was silent except for Meme's feet moving here or there as she busied herself around the house, cleaning, scraping. Her breath seemed to be everywhere around me. I thought that I might eventually just fade away from the sheer boredom of the day, but luckily it was Sunday, which was also bath day. I begrudgingly accepted her offer to let me go first.

To call it a bath was really a stretch. Meme didn't sugar coat it either. "You'll have to be quick," she said, "or freeze doing it." After dinner, she emptied some water from the cistern into the tub and then boiled a couple of pans on the stove until the water was hot enough. Then she poured them into the tub so that the temperature was tepid when I stepped in. It was an old claw foot tub and there were taps on it, but no water came out of them. It didn't take long before the water was gray and my skin shriveled with the cold. I had washed my hair, but it didn't feel entirely clean. This was not a good start.

When I was in bed and Meme climbed up into the loft, I listened as she settled in. "The boy comes back tomorrow. You'll go into school with him to pick up your work and our supplies. The school said they'd work with us this way for the rest of the year because of your...circumstances."

My circumstances. I was already marked. She must've been so embarrassed by me. She didn't even want me to go to school like regular kids my age. The shame of it all.

"No one knows but the school administration," she said. "I want to be clear about that. And no one should know." She didn't want me to talk about what West did, is what she was saying. As if I would. The last thing I needed was for anyone to figure out who I was. Especially him. Marshall. I didn't want him to know how disgusting I was. He was perfect and I was scarred and pebbled. I ran my hands over my arms and felt sick at the touch of my skin. The warmth of my hands on my arms repulsed me. I wanted to claw deep tracks into my arms, but Meme had made me clip my fingernails short.

I thought again of Marshall. His eyes. How he was my link to the outside world. That I would see him again made me feel both sick and excited. He'd only said one word, and yet I felt connected to him. I knew that he had something for me—some knowledge, a lesson—but I didn't yet know what it was. But that couldn't be right. I was probably just being stalkerish. West would have said that to me. "Give it up, Laney," he would've said, back when he used to talk to me. Back when he was my brother.

I lay in bed thinking of the next day, feeling my loneliness and anguish pushing down on me like one of Meme's heavy blankets. Then I remembered that I had a piece of home with me, a connection to the past. When I was sure Meme wasn't going to wake up, I slipped out THE BOOK OF WEST from my duffle bag and removed it from the plastic bag. I held it in my hands and turned on the flashlight I had by the bed. I pulled the blanket up over my head and read.

It started predictably:

Laney, if you are reading this I will kill you!

Seriously, I will hunt you down and cut you if you read this!

I will slit you open like a pig and spread your guts around the yard.

DO NOT READ THIS.

So much for page one. I turned the page in hopes of something more illuminating. The date told me that West started writing this six months or so ago, which was about the time I noticed him skulking around in the woods behind Mrs. Coughlin's backyard.

Despite West's threat, I kept reading. There was nothing he could do to me now.

Mark said I need to quit posting online. He said we needed to go underground. He said we needed to go old school. Ted Kaczynski never had a Reddit account. That dude hated technology. Mark said we needed to put our thoughts down on paper now so that we could create a manifesto. He said we needed to be covert. All of that online stuff we used to do is for amateurs. We're professionals now. We are brothers, he says. We are comrades. Mark listens to me. Mark and I are the same. Psychos and sociopaths.

And we are not like anyone else in this world. WE ARE SPECIAL.

No one else listens to me and everyone sucks. The guidance counselor asks me what's wrong and when I tell her, she asks me if I want to join the LGBT group or whatever. Just because someone calls me a faggot doesn't mean I am one. And really, so what if I was? What's so wrong with being a faggot? At least they aren't fascists like the jocks are. Like Mark said, most of the jocks are going at each other in the shower anyway. Homos!

Mark is so sick. I've never met anyone who is as sick as me. Finally!

He and I used to go online all the time and look up shit on the Taliban. It would be sick to be a member of the Taliban. The United States of Jockmerica needs to die. The Taliban are dedicated to their cause and no one messes with them. What would everyone say if we came into school with big ass beards, wearing white robes? We'd have rifles strapped on to our backs, too.

No one would mess with us then. Those dickheads would be terrified.

We could be suicide bombers. That's so sick! You get on the bus after everyone else and then you hit the button and boom! Everyone dies! Mark is looking into how to build the bombs. He's reading up on Timothy McVeigh and those sickass mothers who bombed the Boston marathon.

That's probably what we'll do. Build bombs and blow everyone up. That would be so sick!!!!!

I hadn't realized that in the hours since I'd been there, I'd been able to put the thought of West's crime out of my head and there he was again, in my head. I didn't know what else I expected to find in this book he'd hidden away. I'd wanted to believe that he'd done something against his will, but his own words showed me the depravity of his soul, the ugliness of his thoughts. I wanted to find sadness and regret, maybe even beauty, but that was not to be found. I guess maybe I hoped he'd say how much he loved me, his sister, but the truth was he never really thought about me at all, just as I'd not thought much about him. Now, I had no choice but to think of him.

His voice and his words clawed and scrambled around in my brain, lodged there. I wondered if his voice would ever go away. I was confused by what I felt because I both missed him and wanted him away. I wanted the old West who was nice to me when we were little kids to come back, but not if that meant the evil West who killed people came with him. I turned off the flashlight and stuffed THE BOOK OF WEST beneath my pillow. Then I took it out from beneath my pillow and put it in the trunk instead. I didn't want it so close to me that it might infect my thoughts as I slept. I wanted it locked away.

Marta had suggested I not watch the television in the days after the murders. She told me not to watch TV or read about the incident in the newspaper. Dumb. Of course, I could find out all I wanted on my phone. I watched victims weeping outside after they escaped from the bus. Newscasters repeated what a miracle it was that anyone survived. "Those boys were intent on killing," one reporter said. "I've never seen such savagery—not even in a war zone. Using the weapons they used—the knives and the machete—made it all the more disturbing. Experts tell us that perpetrators who use these types of weapons are intent on making it a personal act. You have to get close to a person in order to stab him. Chilling."

I saw victims clutching each other and crying. Some looked too shocked to cry. Others were splattered with blood. I saw as emergency crews carried bloodied people out of the bus. Helicopters scanned the area with large lights, looking for the suspect still at large. He is armed and dangerous, the reports said.

There were images of a helicopter circling our house, shining a light down. There was a SWAT team outside, their weapons pointed at our house. Meanwhile, I was inside, oblivious, my headphones on, West pounding on my door. My mother dead.

And then after, when West's and my mother's bodies had been removed from the crime scene and when I was being questioned inside, I saw reporters outside our house, talking about West and our family. Seeing the outside of my house while I was inside was like looking into one mirror while holding up another. You saw yourself over and over again into infinity. There was no escape.

The information overload continued for days. The reporters read from West's old Tumblr. They showed an old family picture of the three of us with Santa—my and Alice's faces were blocked out and only West's visible. I wondered where they'd gotten the photo.

Wondered who'd given it to them. That really bugged me that one of our few friends might have sold us out like that. But then there was no us anymore. It was just me. Sold me out.

I couldn't get enough of the information. I went to West's Facebook page—people had written all sorts of angry and violent messages on his wall. One or two people said that they had always thought he was a nice guy and couldn't believe he'd done it. Some people said they should kill his whole family.

West was a part of us. We must be guilty, too, in some way. I had begun to believe that death might be a good option for me. Might even be the only option. I couldn't see how I could go forward from where I was. Then I realized that maybe forward would never be an option. Maybe I was destined to spend my life looking over my shoulder, standing in place, and hoping for nothing.

Meme shook me awake. I hadn't slept well, thoughts of West crowding into my brain. Then, just when I'd hit the sweet spot of much needed sleep, she was there shaking me. "You've got fifteen minutes to get up and dressed before breakfast," she said. I pulled the cover back over my head. "Get up now," Meme said, pulling it back down. "Marshall will be here shortly." I'd forgotten about him. I was going to be with him again, but alone this time.

I raced about, throwing on clothes, stuffing notebooks, pens, my phone and its charger, into my backpack. I realized, though, that even if my phone was charged, the signal was weak. No matter what, when I was on the bluff, I was on my own. Now was my chance to get out for the day, to breathe in some civilization and enjoy the beauty of electricity and central heating. I was going to school that day to get my work, she'd said. I remembered West's book in the trunk. I definitely didn't want Meme to discover it. I shoved it into the backpack as well.

After breakfast, Meme handed me a paper sack lunch at the

door and reminded me to come right home with Marshall after school. As if I had anywhere else to go. It felt like a long time since I'd been in school, but the reality was that it had only been just over a week. Just over a week and so much had changed already.

I waited on the beach as Marshall crossed the lake. The sun was just barely rising over the mountains when I saw his headlight moving in my direction. I felt exposed standing there. I wasn't sure where I should look—at him, or at my feet. He kept the sled running and his visor down when he pulled up and handed me the helmet. We went through the same routine as the last time and soon crossed the lake. I breathed in deeply, relieved to be away from Meme's bluff and back in what seemed like civilization.

Marshall pulled his sled up to a small house and turned it off. He took off his helmet and I saw that his hair was dark like mine, his skin milky. He had white, white teeth and I wondered if he bleached them. His beauty took my breath away. His beauty was not delicate like my mother's and West's had been. His beauty was strong. Like a horse. Like a stallion. His beauty was thundering. Hooves thundering, shaking the earth beneath my feet. Thundering through my body.

"There's my truck," he said, pointing to a green pickup. "Get in. I'll be out in a second." He went inside to drop off his gear and I got my wits about me and climbed into his truck. I was so cold that I feared I would never warm up.

When Marshall came back out, he carried two travel mugs in his hands and a backpack on his shoulder. He opened the truck and handed me a mug. "Coffee," he said. I didn't tell him that I'd never had coffee. Instead I made a big production of taking a drink of it as he started up the truck. It was so hot that I burned my lip and cried out.

"It's hot," he said, monotone. If I'd known him better, I might've told him he could've warned me, but I didn't. There was something just a little bit scary about him, like he could go off on you at any second. I'd learned not to trust people, males especially. Best to observe and keep quiet before you made up your mind about them, but sitting next to Marshall I wanted to hear him speak. I wanted to know what he thought. I wanted to touch him and have him touch me.

There was so much I wanted to say to him, but also what I felt was beyond words. We drove to school in near silence. Everything I thought to say to him sounded too stupid—like something about the weather or basketball or school. Words kept slipping into my mouth but I couldn't force them out. He didn't even play music, which killed me. I longed to turn on his radio, but wouldn't do that yet. Maybe next time. Maybe next week, or the next.

Weeks and weeks stretched out before me. Would I ever escape from this place and these people? I wasn't sure where to go if I did escape. When we were younger, West and I used to talk about running away, but when we did, we always said we'd run back here, back to Meme. If we'd only known or remembered what it was really like. As we got older we stopped talking about running away together. We stopped talking about Meme except to wonder at her weirdness. Then we stopped talking. I wondered if I'd talked more to West if things would've turned out differently. I wondered if I could've stopped him and saved everyone. If only I'd talked to him or listened.

It took us fifteen minutes to get to the school, which sat just outside of the small town center in what must have been a farmer's field at one time. The wind whipped through the open playing fields, pushing snowdrifts high and higher. The sign out front said: Muskyville Central School.

Marshall pulled into a semi-circular driveway, parked in an empty spot, and cut the engine. "You're supposed to go to the office," he said. He pointed to the doors. "Go in through there. Head down the hall and turn left. You'll see a set off doors. That's the office. Meet me back here after last period." Then he got out of the truck and walked off. Just left me there. Awkward. I looked out at that abandoned playing field and tried to calm the tension in my stomach. Another new school. Not just that: another new school and I didn't know what anyone knew about West. Meme had said nothing, but I wasn't so sure. The news had been national, West's face plastered on every newspaper and television station. My face had not been national, though. It was possible that no one would know about me. It was possible.

I took a deep breath, opened the door to the truck and stepped out into this new world in front of me. I could be new here. I could begin.

Five

The front office ladies gave me my schedule. "You'll have to sit through each class, meet with the teacher, and get your assignment," the older of the two women said to me. "It's all been arranged." She smiled and was about to send me on my way when the principal poked his head out of his office and asked to speak to me. A tall, bearded man, he had a face most people would consider friendly—round, smiling. I entered his office.

"Please have a seat, Elane," he said.

"Laney," I said and sat down, dropping my backpack at my feet.

"Mr. Breck," he said, extending his hand. I was expected to shake it and so I did, nearly gagging at the warm, fleshy feel of his palm. He sat on the edge of his desk, close to where I was sitting in a chair, his crotch at my eye-level. Gross. "I wanted to let you know that we've done our very best to make sure your privacy is intact." I said thank you. "But," he continued, "if anyone bothers you, please let me know immediately. We have a zero tolerance rule for bullying." I nodded and after a few minutes of awkward silence he moved from his spot and paced the room. "What your grandmother has proposed is unorthodox in terms of how you will be taught, but due to your circumstances, we're willing to try it out." Circumstances. There was that word again. He looked at me. "With that said, if you don't complete your work in a timely and appropriate manner, we will have to consider alternatives to your current situation." He must've read my mind because before I could ask him about the alternatives, he told me about them, "Like taking you out of school entirely and having your grandmother teach you strictly from a homeschooling packet," which would mean I wouldn't see Marshall anymore, or not so often, anyway, "or like foster care in a more traditional household." Foster care had not yet entered into the conversation. Had not yet even entered into my mind. I had assumed that if I left my grandmother's house that someone else would take me, but who? I had been stupid. I meant nothing to Marta and Archie was already long gone. I was already living the best alternative, a realization that horrified me. This backwoods life was the best I would get. "Do you understand?" he asked me.

"Yes," I said. I would do my work, but that had never been a problem. I'd always done my work, quietly, efficiently. I had even excelled on occasion, not that anyone noticed or praised me for it. The odd teacher here or there had noticed something special in me, but before I was able to get too close to someone, we'd move on. The cracks had always been around me, and I'd always fallen through them. I learned that no one was there to prop me up. I had to worry about that myself. For years I'd gotten myself up and ready for school. I'd been responsible for my own homework and projects. I'd made my own breakfast and sometimes dinner. I'd done what any other kid whose mother isn't around much does. I took care of myself. I wanted to tell this man that. I wanted to tell him that he didn't really know anything about me.

"But I don't want you to think that you're already being punished, Laney. This is an opportunity and we're all impressed with your transcripts, despite your rather transient lifestyle and other familial issues. All this is to say, we are happy to have you here and we are committed to your education." He smiled, so I smiled back, but mine was forced, holding back the fear clawing up my throat.

A bell rang, signaling that it was time to go to homeroom. I left the office and wandered out into the crowded hall. Other than me, there was one small girl in the class. "Sit here," she said, indicating an empty seat next to her own, and when I did, she turned to me and said, "I'm Zoe." I'd always been suspicious of people who were friendly to me. I felt like they must want something. She was no exception, but she was undeterred by my quiet and chatted on inanely about the school and which teachers were hard and which easy, which mean and which nice. She said we could eat lunch together. She grabbed my schedule and read it over, pointing out the classes we shared—the basics of gym and art. "You're in advanced French," she said, impressed. "I don't do a language."

"I'm not really going to be a full-time student here," I said, but the teacher shushed us before I could explain.

During roll call the teacher had me stand and introduce myself to the class. I kept my head down and mumbled my name as I stood, exposed. I turned my necklace over and around my finger, twisting and untwisting. I might as well have been naked. I couldn't handle how everyone craned around in their seats looking at me. When I sat down, Zoe passed me a note. "You did good!" it said with a smiley face. I wanted to roll my eyes because I thought she was joking, but she was painfully earnest and lacking in the art of sarcasm. This was going to be a long day.

Down the row from where I sat, a lanky, red-haired boy stared at me. He didn't smile or nod or indicate in any way that he was trying to be friendly. I felt like he was trying to pick me apart and examine all of the pieces with his eyes. "What?" I mouthed finally, frustrated. He shrugged, then looked away.

After the bell rang and we all got up to leave, he came over to me. "Do I know you?"

"I've never seen you before," I said, eager to get away. I stood up. Panicked, looking for an escape. He knew me, which meant he knew about me.

"I post school news on Tumblr."

"There's news here?" I didn't know much about the school but I knew that it was small. A central school, it housed 600 K-12 students.

"Some. I'm sure it seems hilarious to you but we do have things happen here."

"What do you mean by that?"

"You look like you've seen things. Been places. Do you have time for an interview?""

"Maybe," I said and turned my head and fussed with my books and moved away from the desk. "But I'm only at school every so often to pick up my assignments." I'd already said too much. I could practically see his dendrites firing as he worked to slot the puzzle pieces together.

After he introduced himself as Craig, he said again, "You really do look familiar." I shifted my head so that my hair would cover my face.

"Maybe you know my grandmother?" I needed to get away from him.

"Hmmm. Maybe," he said to my back as I left the room. "I'll figure out where I've seen you before," he said. "I like a good mystery."

For the rest of the day, I pushed through class after class, meeting with the teachers, accepting their assignments. In each room, I would sit near an outlet and plug in my phone. Once in a while a teacher would notice and ask me to put it away but I was able to get enough of a charge that I could turn it on. I kept on the lookout for Marshall, but only saw him briefly and at a distance during lunch. I looked at him to see if he would wave or smile or acknowledge me in any way, but he didn't seem to see me. I sat with Zoe and her friends and tried to make myself as small as possible so that no one would look at me. I wanted to block it all out—the noise, the lights, the voices, the laughter. It was too normal to be back in school and my life was anything but normal. My hair reeked of wood smoke from the close cabin. The skin on my hands was already chapped and red from the cold. My brain felt bloated and soft in my skull. I wanted out.

For a while I found a quiet stall in the bathroom, locked the door, sat on the toilet and lifted my feet up so no one would see me there. I pulled my newly charged phone out of my bag and slipped my earbuds in. All I wanted to do was listen to some music. As I was fumbling through my playlists, the pressure began. I had forgotten about it all day and now here it was again, to torment me. Another thing for me to hide, lest someone know the freak I really was. I tried to push the pressure away, but it kept coming. The pressure released. Another vision began.

I looked down at bare legs on a toilet seat, and a hand lifting up a stick from between the legs. Covering the stick up with a cover. Looking at the windows on the stick. A plus and a minus. Holding up a box—looking, looking. I could not read the box, could not focus. The hands shook and she thought, What am I going to do? A baby.

A pregnancy test and the results are positive. Breathing fast. Dizzy. Someone else enters the bathroom, closes a stall door. Nothing to do now but flush the toilet. Stuff the test into a backpack. Walk out of the stall. Wash hands, dry them and then turn to the mirror. Her hands smoothed her hair and I knew just who she was. She was young and beautiful and she was my mother. She kept thinking, what am I going to do? She looked so scared. I wanted to tell her not to worry, that it would be all right. She would make it.

But I stopped myself thinking that. It wasn't all right. It wasn't okay. Don't keep the baby, I tried to tell her. Get rid of it.

She blinked, almost like she heard me. She touched the cross at her neck. She rubbed it.

A baby, she thought. My own baby. Someone to love only me.

My baby.

Love and longing washed over me. I wanted it. I wanted to keep it.

After the vision passed, I stayed in the stall for a long time thinking about how she must've felt. I was shaking, but not with cold. My whole body felt sick and beaten and I was exhausted by the sadness of it all. She was in high school. In this high school, not much older than me, and she was pregnant with West. I hadn't ever known how scared she was and how much she gave up to have us, until now. I thought of her hands on my cheeks, wiping away my tears when I cried over skinning my knee. Her hand in my hair when I was too scared to sleep at night. Those hands were my hands now. Whenever I had a vision of her, I became her. It was almost as good as having her back and yet different. I was learning what it felt like to be her. Learning, maybe, about why she'd been the way she'd been and seeing the world through her eyes. If only I had had these visions while she was still alive. I could've said something to her. I could've told her how much I understood. I could've forgiven her.

At the end of day, I headed out to the parking lot to meet up with Marshall. Exhausted from having to hold in my emotion all day, I wanted to get inside the truck and have a quiet ride home but a quiet ride was not meant to be. As I approached the truck, I saw them: Marshall leaning with his back against the hood, his arms crossed over his chest. In front of him was a miniscule, blonde girl. She had to be half my height and weight. She was adorable, childlike, but also womanly. I loathed her immediately. He was gazing down at her, listening as she spoke. Then he bent and kissed her on the top of her head. Depressed at the sight of them, I nearly walked off in the other direction, but I was riveted. I wanted it to be me he kissed, but then I knew that it never would be. Of course he had a beautiful girlfriend. Boys like him always did. Why did I expect things to be otherwise? I would never be his girlfriend.

Then Marshall noticed me standing there. He said something to the girl and she turned her pretty face to see me. She gave a little wave. "Hi-iii," she said in a baby voice.

I walked over. "I'm Linda," she said, waving some more.

"Let's go," Marshall said and she rolled her eyes, swatting at him with one of her tiny pink hands.

"His manners suck," she said. We got in the truck then, me on one side, Marshall on the other, and little Linda in between us. "We're cousins," she said. "You and me." She pointed at me. I didn't know I had cousins. "Your mother is my father's second cousin, which makes us... What does it make us?" She looked to me as if I would know. "Anyway," she said. "We're blood." And then she laughed. I hadn't anticipated that I would have relatives up there other than Meme. It was odd, not something I had experienced before—to be connected to someone by blood other than your immediate family. West and I hadn't experienced that. Alice kept us away from any relations. She kept us on the move. She'd always been running away, but we never knew from what.

I watched Linda's pretty hands as they plucked at the radio dial. Her fingernails were perfectly shaped and clean. I looked at my own, dirty and cracked. "Dude," she said, flicking off the radio in disgust. "This thing is so old school. You even have a cassette player. Do you know I had to ask my dad what a cassette player is? My dad!" She laughed. My mother had listened to mixed tapes in her car. Old ones from when she was my age. That was part of the reason, other than money, that she'd never gotten a new car. "How will I listen to my tapes?" she asked no one.

Soon we were driving in the opposite direction of the lake. Linda talked on and on, asking me questions about where I was from, what I did there, what music I liked—not that she waited for my responses. I learned that she was a cheerleader and into drama. I learned that she liked to snowboard and ride motorbikes.

Marshall pulled into the driveway of a tidy farmhouse and

got out of the truck. Linda scooted along the seat after him and waved bye to me. I sat facing forward as they stood in the driveway talking. Then he hugged her. I felt ashamed and alone. I wanted my mother beside me to tell me it would be okay, that there would be another boy that I liked as much as this one. But she had never been that sort of mother. So I told this to myself: someday you will find a boy you like just as much or maybe even more than this one. I knew it wasn't true, though.

From the first time I saw him, I knew he was the one.

Marshall drove me across the lake on his snowmobile. He called it his sled. "See you next week," I said over the engine. He nodded without removing his helmet. The helmet seemed symbolic of our ability to communicate with each other or not. My words would always buck up against the barrier of his silence. I thought about what I might say to him the next time I saw him. I could tell him about what it was like living with Meme, but that might be boring. I could tell him about how I was going to learn how to track animals, but maybe he would think that was stupid. It was useless. I was boring and had nothing interesting to say. I should just keep my mouth shut. I walked up the path. The sun was creeping down toward the mountains as I entered the quiet house. I called out for Meme but there was no response. She was out somewhere. Everything was still. No furnace tick or television voices in the background. Only the soft hum of the propane refrigerator and the crack of wood burning in the stove. I felt like an intruder standing there, alone.

For the past days, I had wanted nothing more than to be alone in the house, so that I might examine things more closely and now I had my opportunity. Of particular interest to me was a roll-top desk in the corner. I tried to pull down the lid, but it was locked. I opened each of the drawers, but didn't find the key. Never mind. I could find it later.

I gave up my search and went up into the loft. Meme had made my bed and left a note on it saying, "Tomorrow this is your job." I'd never had to make my bed before. It wasn't something Alice expected us to do. Cleaning, in general, was not her strong suit, though I struggled to think what had been her strong suit the last few years. The longer I stayed in this house, the less I felt I'd ever known my mother. I hadn't really known what she loved or how she felt until now, thanks to these visions. I wished she'd been able to share herself with me like that instead of me finding out all this stuff after she was gone. It wasn't fair.

I sat on the bed and dumped my backpack on the floor. I had the whole week to work on my assignments, but I felt a sense of urgency to get stuff done. I thought of school, the faces and sounds and smells from the day washing over me. I remembered that there was an old fashioned phone booth in the front lobby. Now that my phone was charged, I took it out and looked at the face. Only one bar that flickered in and out. Still, I would call someone. Maybe Archie. I had him in my contacts. I never thought I'd think this but it would've been nice to hear his voice, the familiarity of it. Before I could decide what to do, the bar flickered out and no service flashed on the screen. I held the button down until the phone turned off. Tomorrow, I would go out into the woods and see if I could find a spot with better service.

As I was sitting there, I thought of something I wanted to tell West about the day. About how that kid who wanted to interview me for the paper, and wasn't that hilarious? I sat up and made to get off the bed to find him before I caught myself. I didn't want to think about him so much. At least he had always been there to commiserate with when things were really bad. He should've been with me at Meme's, for instance. We could've talked about how much it sucked to live in the middle of nowhere.

I slumped onto the floor. My backpack was next to me. I put

my hand inside it and rubbed against the cover of THE BOOK OF WEST. I didn't want to read any more of it. I wanted to remember West they way he used to be, way back when we were kids. He protected me then. He took care of me. I didn't want to know this West, but I didn't know how to stop myself from reading more. I had to wait until later, though, when Meme was asleep. I couldn't risk her finding out. I turned to look out the window. Something red on the floor caught my eye. Alice's notebooks.

I picked one up and flicked through it. Halfway through the equations gave way to words. Words upon words, scrawled in Alice's loopy, unmistakable cursive. This was the book I had seen her hands writing in my vision.

In this first notebook there was only one entry, an unfinished letter:

Dear Ben,

I sometimes feel like I don't want to have this baby. I feel like I want to have you all for myself and not share you with anyone, not even my own child. But then I know that this baby is part of us—part of you and part of me and because of that this baby will be beautiful and perfect.

I know that my mother hates me for what I've done and I know everyone else thinks that they're right that we're too young to try to manage on our own but I believe that we can do it if we put our minds to it. We can do anything. I know YOU are strong enough to take care of a family. I know I am.

I'm not far enough along yet to show or to feel the baby kicking or anything but I know that it is alive inside me. I can feel it. My mother told me she would like me to give the baby away. She says what do I know about mothering? But I know I can do better than my mother did. I know it. I wish she would just give me a chance. Will you ask her to give me a chance? Will you tell her how much we love each other?

Can you picture what our family will be like? Maybe we'll have a son and a daughter and live in a nice little house in town. We can play baseball and have picnics. It will be everything I never had. Everything you never had.

Being your wife is all I have ever wanted. When can we be married? I honestly don't think I can live without you, or should I say, I don't want to live without you. I can't live without you. Please don't ever leave me. Promise you won't.

The passage ended there and the rest of the notebook was empty. Those words must've been why Meme kept it. They must've tortured her and they should have. She pushed her own daughter to give up a child. She turned her back. I couldn't wait to confront her with what I knew, but not yet. I would save my outrage for when I needed it.

I held the notebook for a long time before the door finally opened. Meme stomped into the room, knocking the snow off her boots.

"Hello?" she called out.

I thought about not responding but yelled out anyway, "I'm here."

"Good," she said. "It's time to get ready for dinner."

I went down the ladder and saw that there was stuff on the table—cutlery, plates, napkins-—but it was not set. "That's your job," Meme said without turning around from the pot she was stirring. "Set the table, please."

I placed the napkins and cutlery, the plates and cups. As I did, I noticed a pack of cigarettes in the center of the table. I didn't think she smoked. Exactly. She never smoked. Then I realized those cigarettes were mine.

"Found those while I was putting away your things," Meme said. She carried the pot to the middle of the table and headed back to the stove for hot rolls. "There's no smoking in my house."

My face was burning hot—not just because I was embarrassed, but also because I was furious. "You had no right to go through my things," I said, snatching the cigarettes up from the table.

She turned from the stove with the rolls in her hand and walked slowly to the table, put them down. She took the oven mitts off her hands. "My house," she said, grabbing the cigarettes from me, "my rules. Your mother might have thought it was okay to let you kids do whatever you want, but I do not. You will follow my rules." She twisted the pack and balled it up as best she could. "And these things will kill you."

"Maybe I want to die," I said. I ran up into the loft, away from her. I heard her sighing, mumbling about silly girls, as I hit my bed. What did she know? She was a crazy, rabbit-killing old lady. She didn't know what the smell of smoke meant to me. It was like my mother was right there with me. When I smelled it, I smelled her.

I stayed there until the light leeched out of the sky and stars pushed through. Then I pulled the covers over my head and took out the flashlight and read from West's book:

Mark thinks it will be too risky if we continue to research online. He thinks the FEDERAL GOVERNMENT will be after us—possibly even the secret service—if we do. He said we need to be more sneakier about this operation.

He said we'd record our manifesto and post it on YouTube right before we act. I told him hell yeah. That would be sick!

So that's what we're going to do. Then afterwards, when we're gone, everyone will know what we stood for. Everyone will know that we hate all pig-eating Americans, especially those that go to our stupid school.

If only we could get out of here. We talked about running away—just stealing some money and backpacking around Europe. I still think about that idea...

One of the people who was seriously injured in the attack was Mrs. Yello, my English teacher. She was signed up as a chaperone for the trip. She was young and everyone really liked her. Mrs. Yello was always nice to me. Encouraging. She said, "You're a good writer, Laney," and I believed her. She told me to keep writing. To put my thoughts down. "Someday maybe you'll write a book," she said, "and if you do, I'll be first in line to buy it." She'd just gotten married the year before and was pregnant. She lost the baby in the attack. She lived, though. Mrs. Yello lived.

I thought about what her life would be like now. I wondered if she would ever teach again or try to have another baby. I wondered if she hated me. I thought of getting in touch with her, writing her a letter and telling her how sorry I was that this had happened. Maybe someday I would do it. Reach out to her and see if she reached back to me. We were connected in this grief, after all, and this anger. But I wasn't sure if sorry was enough of a thing to say to her. I wasn't sure if my sorry would matter.

I turned off the flashlight and stared into the dark. West's and Alice's voices were reaching out to me past time and space. Through the darkness and into the darkness. I wanted to feel silence spreading across me like ice. I wanted the ice to form a hard crust around me, impenetrable, where no voices, no visions, could reach me.

I woke up in the dark on top of the covers. The only sound was Meme's snoring behind the curtain. Starving, I went downstairs using my flashlight and found that she had left food for me. A peanut butter and honey sandwich, which is my favorite. How did she know? Next to the sandwich, a note: "No Smoking!"

I switched off my flashlight and ate my sandwich. I was starving, so I didn't mind that the honey had crystallized and gone crunchy. The only sounds were the ticking clock and the wind pushing snow across the lake, swaying the trees, scattering clouds across the bright crescent moon.

I wondered if it was dark where my mother and father and West were. I wondered if they knew where they were. I wondered if they would always know what West had done. I wondered if they missed me. Or was there just nothing?

Just velvet blackness. No stars. No hot breath melting frost from a windowpane. Nothing.

The next morning, I began my education according to my grandmother. This meant I was to do all of the housework she required of me, sweeping, peeling, scrubbing, washing, and dumping, and then sit for several hours with my work assignments, and then spend another couple of hours carrying in armloads of wood for the stove. Once everything was completed to her satisfaction, she told me it was time for exercise. "To live out here like this you need to be both mentally and physically fit," she said. Great. I'd never been sporty, but I enjoyed the woods back home, though I'd never been one to travel far from the boundaries of my yard. Here the boundaries seemed limitless. As thrilling as that was, it was also terrifying.

It was cold unlike any cold I had remembered, but dressed in hand-me-down clothes I was warm enough to spend a few hours outside. Meme gave me instruction on an old pair of snowshoes. She strapped them on over the boots she'd given me. "Put one foot in front of the other and walk like normal," she said. She'd given me poles to poke into the ground as I walked. I walked a few feet and then stopped. "Come on back," she said.

I turned my body as best I could and looked at her. "I don't know how to turn around," I said.

"Put your right foot into a T-shape with your left foot and then put your left foot parallel. Continue this until you have turned." I did as she said and made my way back in her direction. "There," she said. "Wasn't that easy?" It was sort of easier than I'd expected, but my thighs were already burning and I'd hardly gone anywhere yet.

"I don't suppose you know how to use a compass?" she asked.

"There's a GPS on my phone," I said, gasping from the exertion.

She snorted. "That'll do you no good here," she said. "More

fools get lost in the woods because of those things, costing taxpayers ungodly amounts of money to rescue them." Enraged, she shook her head. "For today, you stick close to the shoreline, walk for thirty minutes, and then follow your tracks back. I'll teach you about the compass another time." Then she turned and walked away from me. "Be back before sundown," she called back to me without turning around. I stood there until the crunch of her boots on the snow was gone.

I was alone. Just me and the trees and the wind. A crow called out from the opposite shore, but it sounded clear, as though it were right next to me. Sound carried in extraordinary ways in that bowl of frozen water and mountains. I began my trek. I'd brought my useless phone regardless. At least it would keep time. She said to walk for thirty minutes. I could've walked for a few minutes and told her I'd walked thirty, but I had a feeling she'd know if I lied. I set a timer on the phone. I hoped to find a signal out here, but if I didn't, I was used to carrying my phone and still felt wrong whenever it wasn't with me. But even if something went wrong, who was there to call? Meme had no phone. And if Marshall had one, I didn't know his number. There was always 911 but how would I explain to them where to find me? With that realization, it finally sunk in how fully I was on my own.

I moved forward on the snowshoes as my grandmother had taught me to. I moved out onto the ice and followed the shoreline. All I heard was the crunch of my feet, the crack of my poles through the crust of the snow, the distant crows, my breath. After a while, I forgot to be scared that I was out there alone. That I was away from anyone who might save me. That I didn't need saving. I thought of my mother here, as a girl, possibly walking in these same snowshoes, following this same shore. I stopped and breathed in, letting my shaking thighs rest. I took my water bottle from my backpack and drank deeply. The sun was high and the snow sparkled. Swirls of snow rose from the tops of the mountains to my west. Across the lake, a dog barked once and no more. I stood for a long time and just looked at all around me, and listened.

Soon, I began walking again, pushing through the pain. Before I knew it, the timer on my phone buzzed. I'd not made it as far as I thought I would, but I would do better tomorrow and the next day and the day after that. I would be faster and better. I turned as Meme had taught me to and headed back to her house, to home. When I got there, the sun was beginning to descend westward, the sky bright red and pink, glorious. I realized as I stood and watched it push downward that I'd not once thought to take a picture with my phone as I might've done in the past. There was no one in the world I wanted to share it with. This sky was for me alone.

Time passed with our rhythm of days and everything began to seem just a bit more normal to me. All of the ways that had seemed unfathomable when I first moved in with my grandmother were now routine. It was strange how easily I'd given up the comforts I was used to in exchange for the hard work required to keep us warm and fed. I would never admit it to anyone, but I'd grown to almost like life on the bluff.

Even school wasn't bad. My trips there would've been tolerable, even pleasurable, because I got to be near Marshall, but for one person: Craig. He was relentless. Every time I turned around, there he was. "I Googled you," he said, and I gave him back the blank stare I had been practicing since the incident. "I turned up nothing," he said, "but you probably already knew that. I'm guessing you are under an assumed name. Maybe even the witness protection program?" I was at the locker the front office had assigned me, and turned from him to gather my books for my next class.

"I'm going to be late," I said as I turned to leave. He kept pace with me. I stopped walking and faced him. I said, "Why don't you leave me alone?"

"I'll leave you alone if you'll sit down for an interview," he said. "Nothing major. Just questions about where you're from and why you're here." The old me would've told him to go to hell, but I was wary of him and my gut told me not to make him an enemy.

"I'll think about it," I said.

I saw Marshall up ahead, watching us. He caught my eye and nodded. I nodded back and tried not to smile. He seemed to be everywhere and nowhere at this school. The announcements in the morning were all about his achievements on the basketball court, but whenever I had looked for him in the halls, he was nowhere to be found. It seemed that only when I gave up looking for him did he appear.

I slipped into my class just before the bell rang and spent the rest of the time daydreaming about Marshall to take my mind off Craig.

At the end of the day, I waited for Marshall's truck. I'd turned in my assignments and was loaded up for the next week. He had told my grandmother that sometimes we'd be late getting home because he had practice. The two of them had no problem talking. It was only with me that he was silent.

I looked out at the playing fields, and the farm fields, and the forest beyond that. Snow drifted across the empty spaces. I was so deep in thought that I didn't notice that Marshall was there, getting into his truck, turning it on. We drove back over the roads we'd traveled a few hours earlier, back onto his sled and across the lake. All in silence.

As I got off his sled and said thank you, he held out a hand and grabbed my arm. "Wait," he said. He took off his helmet. "That kid. Craig?" I nodded. "He likes to stir stuff up. He's not a bad guy, though. Just nosy. Don't let him get to you."

"I won't," I said.

"Good," Marshall said. He'd noticed me during the day and he cared enough to comment on something that might be bothering me. He put his helmet on and drove away, leaving me standing there, breathless.

I pushed open the door at home expecting to see Meme by the fire and instead I found her sitting at the table with Chellie, drinking coffee and laughing.

"There she is," Meme said, her cheeks were flushed and she looked beautiful and young, happy. "Come in, Elane," Meme said. "Come sit with us." I took off my coat and reluctantly sat. "Chellie's here to check in," Meme said. "And to bring some supplies."

"Marta said to say hi," Chellie said. I winced at the sound of her name. Marta. It felt like a million years since I'd seen her. "I'm supposed to report back to her. Let her know you're doing okay. I, uh, need to take your picture," Chellie said. "She needs it for her records." She had me stand next to my grandmother. I suppose I should've smiled but my face was stone. Chellie took a photo with her phone and stored it to email later. She showed it to me before putting her phone away. "You look like mother and daughter," she said. I smirked, but I knew she was right. The way we looked, Meme could've been a mother to me.

It was weird having someone else in the room with us. This was our space. I didn't like it. Not one bit. I wanted her gone. They small talked with me for a while, asking about school. My responses were terse, monosyllabic. Meme sighed. "I told you," she said. "The girl is no great conversationalist."

Chellie laughed. "You used to say the same thing about me when I was that age."

"That doesn't seem possible now seeing what a chatty Cathy you are." Meme was smiling with her, pleasant in a way I'd not yet seen. When she turned back to me, her face was hard. "Elane, put away the groceries, please." To compensate for whatever Meme had not canned or put up herself—coffee, sugar, that sort of thing—Chellie brought supplies every so often. I'd wondered where the food would come from. Our supplies seemed to be dwindling. "I might need to order more often," she said. "This child is eating me out of house and home." I blushed.

"I didn't see a sled," I said to hide my embarrassment. Chellie pointed to snowshoes leaning against the wall.

"I parked in the driveway at the skidoo club and hiked in on the logging road," she said. The road. They had all said it was impassable in winter, but they meant cars. Suddenly the world opened up just a little bit more.

I helped to unpack the groceries and then left them. My bed was the only space I seemed to have as my own. I retreated there whenever I felt lost, as I did then. I lay down and tried to push the day away. Craig, Marshall's silence and then his words, and now this other person down below. Soon the pressure picked up and pulsed at my temples. It was happening again. I tried not to let fear overtake me and just breathed into it.

I heard water and felt the sun. I was on a boat, on a lake. A man was next to me, talking. I breathed and his words came into focus. "I'm sorry," he said. "It's not that I don't love you. I just can't deal with this right now, Al. We can't be parents. I can't be a dad. I don't feel ready for it. I'm sorry."

There was a pain like a stab in my stomach and a fire in my chest, but the pain wasn't necessarily physical. It was emotional. He was breaking up with me. I couldn't speak. Wouldn't speak.

I put the boat into full throttle and we lurched forward. The man fell back. I knew where I was headed. I pulled up quickly, dangerously at a dock. He used to like it when I was dangerous. He grabbed onto the dock. "Please. Can't you just say something?" He grabbed at my hands on the wheel. I pulled them away.

"Yes," I said, breathing hard so that I would not cry. He must not see me cry. "I can say something. I can say that I never want to see

*you again, Ben." He looked hurt but complied and climbed onto the
deck. "Give me a push off," I said. I was tough as nails. I was dying
inside.*

*He pushed the boat and I turned the wheel. "Wait," he yelled
after me. "Alice! Please wait."*

*I was crying now. Heading away from him. The wind pushed
the tears back across my cheeks. I had not given him what he wanted
and he'd left me. My heart would never heal from this wound.*

I woke up later, afraid and lonely. He had broken up with her.
He had tried to change the course of things but she wouldn't listen.
The break up couldn't have lasted long, otherwise I wouldn't have
been here, alive. I wanted to talk to my mother and tell her about
all that I was seeing, her past life.

She would've laughed at me. Told me I was thinking too
much. Told me I was tired or that I was being too sensitive. "My
thoughtful child," she used to say to me. "My thinker."

I wanted her voice, though not as it was in the visions. I wanted
it the way it had been when she was alive. I wanted her near. I still
had one of Alice's notebooks and the yearbook that I hadn't looked
at yet. I almost didn't want to. I was afraid that they might be empty
or filled only with her schoolwork. I wanted to find her again in the
pages. I had placed them in a drawer in my nightstand. I figured
that Meme had already read them. I opened the nightstand and
pulled out the green notebook. On the cover was Alice's name and
ENGLISH in block letters. Inside, there was one paragraph about
Shakespeare's THE TEMPEST on the first page and then nothing
for a few pages. On the fifth page, she wrote again:

*School is done for me. I can't go back there. Ben has left. Gone
back down state to his people there. He may never return. I don't
know. I can't breathe when I think about him being gone.*

*I'm too tired to carry on. This baby wears me out and I haven't
even had it yet. I thought that I could do it, but I can't. Everyone stares
at me and my belly. Everyone whispers behind my back. Teachers*

look at me like I am bad news—the same teachers who used to tell me about scholarships and opportunities. It seems all of my choices come down to this one. I will have this baby and keep him and if that means that all of the other doors slam shut, so be it.

My mother has told me she will teach me here at home. Just her and me. We will carry on, she says. Forget about him, she says.

By him, she means Ben. But I can't forget him. He is what I live for.

I wonder what would've happened if he and I had never met? Where would I be now? I would certainly be lonelier. My mother thinks we're ruining our lives. She says she's not just worried about my life but about his life, too. I don't believe her. "You have a bright future, Alice," she says. "I wish someone had told me that when I was your age," she says. "Go out and live," she says.

But I don't want to live if there is no Ben to live with. If I don't have him, I just want to die. I wonder if Ben feels the same way about me that I do about him. Can he? Is it possible to love as much as I love? I must get him back. I'll do anything to keep him. I will.

Alice felt no closer to me. In fact, she felt farther away. I wished that I might call her to me in another vision, but it didn't seem to work that way. The visions just happened. I was not in control of them. It was like Alice's love of Ben. She didn't control it because it was in control of her. I never wanted to feel like that, but it might have made me feel better to love someone that way. Maybe I would feel less alone.

I thought of Marshall. I thought of his lips, what would they feel like on mine. I thought of the warmth of his cheek. I thought of the way his eyes reflected back the sky. If I loved him, I would be strong about it. If I loved him, I would not need. If I loved him.

But I knew nothing of love.

Here were the facts:

Fact: I had never been in love before.

Fact: I had never kissed anyone I loved before.

Fact: West's evil friend Mark tried to do something to me. I've never told anyone this, but it's true.

What he did to me felt horrible and ugly and left me feeling ashamed. I never told anyone about it because I was scared what he would do to me if I did. I was also scared what other people would think of me. What West would think of me and do to me if I told. I never told.

Here's what happened: It was another Friday night. I was home, as I always was on Friday nights. I had one or two friends, but only at school. No one bothered with me otherwise. No one wondered about my life. It was like I ceased to exist when I left school, not that I existed much while I was there. When I was a little kid I thought I'd always feel happy as long as I had my mother and West, but each year I realized that wasn't true. Even with them, I was alone. Neither of them ever fully committed to being a part of the family I envisioned.

So, I was home and I thought I was alone and so didn't worry that I would bump into anyone when I made my way to the bathroom dressed only in a t-shirt and underwear. The hall was dark when I came back out of the bathroom, which was funny because I thought I'd left the light on. I reached my hand out for the wall and the switch, when I felt a hand on my wrist, twisting it back behind me. Another hand over my mouth, pulling me, pushing me. I was back in the bathroom and Mark was there with me, pushing me against him with a hand on my back.

He said, "Don't say anything or I'll kill you." He showed me a knife. His eyes stared into mine and I couldn't tell whether he hated me or not. Honestly, it looked like he was beyond hate. Like he wasn't capable of emotion.

He was up so close to me that I could see his pitiful beard growing in. His breath steamed up his glasses. "I'm going to take my hand off your mouth and you will kiss me. Okay?" he said. And when I didn't respond, he asked me again. I nodded. My body and mind went into a dark brown space, a cave, where I felt no emotion, only the instinct to survive.

He took his hand off my mouth and I tightened my lips together as I would've done if someone tried to feed me something unpleasant to eat. He pushed his face close to my face and plastered his mouth against mine. He kissed me, if that is what you want to call it. With his mouth, he forced my mouth open. His hand reached down and lifted up my shirt. He grabbed at my breasts. I tried to squirm away, but he held me tight.

Then I heard West call from the other room. "Dude, you've got to come see this." Mark stopped what he was doing.

"I'll be right there," he yelled. Then he whispered to me, "Remember, keep quiet or I'll kill you."

I was familiar with that threat. I'd heard such a threat before, from my brother. And just like West, I knew Mark wasn't lying.

I found that I needed to push all of these ugly thoughts away. I heard my grandmother down below, cooking the meal, Chellie long gone. Instead of hearing my mother's or West's voice, I needed to hear my own. I picked up the book nearest me and began reading. Instead of letting them dwell within me, I would learn. "No one can take your education away from you," Meme had said to me the day before. "Not one person."

At first I read *Mammal Tracks and Sign: A Guide to North American Species* to pass the time, but as I read on, I found the book made more sense to me. It was a lot like what was going on inside my head with the visions. The book gave me a new perspective from which to view the world. I learned how to use tracks and scat to determine the animal. Yes, this was exactly what my life had come to. This was how I entertained myself now that I was become handier on the snowshoes—I sought out animal scat in the woods. I'll admit it was a weird hobby, but you find yourself doing weird stuff when you're trapped in the woods in the winter with no other source of entertainment.

To begin with tracking, you examine the track from three perspectives—lying, standing, and flying. Lying down is when you get all close and personal with your track, planting your nose as near it as possible. Standing allows you to take a look at the trail, not just the track. Flying is when you use what you know of the surrounding ecology to bring perspective to the track. Also important is whatever it is that the animal has stepped in, like mud or snow. How deep the animal steps determines the size and shape of its track.

Basically, you look for signs: When you see some tracks you are to get down on the ground and examine the area from a low vantage point, from that of an animal. Look up at the sky, what do you see? Look ahead, what's there? You measure the tracks. You examine them. How many toes and toe pads? What shape are the feet? Has its body left a mark on the snow? Are there signs the animal has eaten any vegetation? If so, at what level? Are there signs of fur?

All of these are clues for finding out what your animal is. You might, for example, think that you've found the tracks of a wolverine in the snow, only to discover that it was a bullfrog up too early from his winter nap.

As I read, I also learned that the book had once belonged to my mother. Her name was written in the front cover and throughout she'd written notes to herself in the margin. There were also folded-up sketches of tracks stuffed in between the pages. As I read, though, the book became less about her and more about me. Following an animal's tracks and trying to determine what kind of animal it was and where it was going was like getting into its head and understanding the world from its perspective. It was like seeing the world through the eyes of another. Now that I actually did see the world that way from time to time, in a way that was beyond my control, I wanted to learn to see the world through the eyes of another in a way I could control.

So this was what I did: I put all of my winter clothes on and the thick hooded parka Meme had given me. I put my book and notebook in my backpack. Downstairs, she stopped me on my way out. "It'll be dark soon," she said.

"I'm only going for a while," I said. "I need some exercise." I'd yet to master the compass and so she warned me to mark my way back and not get lost. She warned me, again, to stay near the shore so that I could use it as my marker. "I know, I know," I said, exasperated. I wanted away from her and everything.

She said everything you would think a mother would say to you, but mine never had.

The woods in winter were more beautiful than I thought they would be. Across the lake, I heard a chain saw, a truck starting, the plaintive bark of a dog. From the shore, I could track with my eyes the path Marshall and I hadn't taken earlier that day, even in the fading light.

Meme had warned me that by late March the lake might be impossible to cross. She told me I might have to stay home with her for a few weeks before we could take the boat out on the water.

"We'll listen," she said. "And the lake will tell us when it's time." I had no idea what she meant by this, but I'd learned that she wasn't exactly the clearest person sometimes, so I just nodded and murmured my agreement. Meme had taken more and more to calling me my mother's name and when I questioned her about it, she looked at me like I was crazy. I said, "I'm not Alice, you know," and she replied, "I know that. I'm not a damn fool!" Often, I would hear her talking to someone and when I entered the room, expecting to find someone else there, she was alone. Either we had ghosts, or she was losing her mind. Neither thought appealed to me. But this was also why the woods became my place of safety when I was home.

The woods. My feet coasted over the top of the snow and my breath huffed out and out and out. I stopped and held my breath long enough to listen and look. A tree branch up high cracked. Snow drifted down. The sun pushed quickly down toward the horizon. Soon it would be dark. I could stand still and chart its path if I wanted. There was no reason to do anything else than that. As I had done so many times since that night, I wondered what if I had been in that bus—not that I would have been, because I was not associated with basketball, but still I wondered what if some fluke had caused me to be there.

I thought of the last time I saw West. Early on his last night, he came to my room and knocked on the door. When I opened the door, he asked, "You going to the game?"

"Yeah, right," I said and rolled my eyes.

"Don't go, okay?" he said.

"Since when do you care what I do?" I asked, but he moved away from me, my question hanging between us unanswered.

As I stood there in the woods, I felt him moving away from me in the same way he had been that night. If only I'd stopped him and made him answer me and tell me what he planned to do. I could've done something if only I'd made him talk to me. I could've talked him out of it. If he wouldn't listen to me, I could've called the police. If the police didn't listen to me, I could've gone into the bus and raised my voice and warned everyone to get out. I could've saved them if only I had made him stop and talk to me.

I found a boulder near the shore, took off the snowshoes and climbed up the rock until I was on a flat part at the top. I took out my tracking book and my journal. I meant to write about what I'd seen already—more squirrel tracks, something dog-like, possibly coyote—but instead of pulling out my journal, I pulled out two things I had brought with me: THE BOOK OF WEST and Alice's yearbook.

The yearbook had an embossed cover and inside in the back

and front were inscriptions to Alice. All about what a great friend she was. How pretty she was. How much fun. Girls signed their names telling Alice how much they loved her. Boys joked around and flirted. I paged through the photos. I found a few of Alice taken candidly. In one she sits in a classroom and as the camera catches her, she turns to it and sticks out her tongue.

There was a photo of her at her junior prom. She was not with my father, but instead dancing with another boy. They both have crowns on their heads. She was the prom queen. There was a photo of them kissing beneath an enormous, fake crescent moon.

There was a photo of her lined up with the volleyball team. And one as she served the volleyball, her hair arcing out behind her.

She was everywhere.

It seemed impossible to me that this pretty, popular girl could be the same person who was my mother. It seemed impossible that this same person created me and West. She must've expected so much more from us. What a disappointment we both must have been. So antisocial and weird.

I looked at these photos of Alice as a younger person and wondered how it was that I came to be. Were all of my bits and pieces in there just waiting to come out? And then I started to wonder forward at how someday, maybe my own kid would look at a photo of me and wonder the same things. All of this wonder catapulted me into infinity and made me feel less alone. These bits of me would carry on into the world and into the darkness.

THE BOOK OF WEST waited for me, almost an antidote to the sweetness of my mother's yearbook. I'd been trying not to read it anymore. Trying to pretend it didn't exist or that West never existed. Trying to pretend I could be this new girl.

But there it was in my hands, clawing at me, desperate for my attention, and so I opened it and read:

They had me on Xanax for anxiety and now Lexapro for

depression. Neither seems to make a bit of difference. It's not that I'm not depressed anymore, it's that I'm dulled or something. Drowsy. Everything feels pillowed over. I hate it. I want to feel things again and right now all I feel is that I don't want to wake up one more day and be living this stupid, pointless life. I want to die and take as many of you with me as I can.

No one loves me and I love no one. If they could all just jump inside my body for one minute and know how bad it feels to be me, how much it hurts. Someday I will show you. Someday you will know.

I want you all to feel what I feel. All of the pain and the horror. I hate you. I hate you all.

I HATE YOU.

West had written with such force that his pen dug through the page. I turned the page and felt the imprint for several pages afterward. There were drawings on the pages—knives dripping blood. Screaming people. Guns shooting. His drawings were rudimentary, pitiful, like the drawings of a small, angry child. I took off my glove and ran my finger over one of them.

He drew this picture and now he is dead. He wrote these words and now he is dead. He will never feel the cold air or the sunlight again.

I had no stomach for more reading after that and no stomach for more tracking. West had stolen the day from me once again. I would head back to Meme, who was the only person worried about where I might be in the world, and the warm fire waiting for me.

I surprised myself by finding my way back to the house by the light of the moon. Back home I would have used a flashlight but my eyes had become accustomed to the lack of extra light. It was like I could see without using my eyes sometimes. I was learning to find my way through these woods. I was learning to find my way home.

As I walked in the door and stomped off my boots, there was Meme, setting food out on the table. "You're back," she said, turning to me and smiling with affection. "I was about to send a search party out for you." We both laughed because we knew that if I were lost, she was the only one who would come looking for me. "Time to eat," she said.

Six

"This place does not run by itself," Meme told me the next day after breakfast. I'd been doing well with keeping up with homework and the chores she'd given me, but apparently, there was more to come. So much so that by Wednesday, I was usually finished with all that needed to be done. It was the housework where she felt I was slacking. "I've gone easy on you up until now, but now it's time you pull your weight. It's time for you to learn the most important lesson of living out here with me. Do you know what that is?" I stared at her, mulling over possible answers, each more snarky than the next. I kept my mouth shut instead.

She stood up and paced the room. "We are the water," she said. "We are the electricity and the lights. We are the food, and we are most definitely the heat." Basically, she was reiterating what I already knew—if we wanted something to happen, we needed to make it happen ourselves. We needed to be self-reliant. If we want heat, we must chop and pile the wood. Then we must bring the wood from the pile into the house and get it into the stove and the fireplace.

After we dressed and went outside. "You're going to learn how to chop wood," she said. She showed me how to place the wood, standing up on one end, on top of the big stump she had for splitting. Then she taught me how to use the axe, swinging it from behind onto the center of the piece of wood. Once we had a cut in the wood, she showed me how to insert the wedge, using the other side of the axe to pound it in. Then I was to hit the wedge with the axe blade. It took me a few tries to get it right.

"You're strong," she said after I had split many pieces. "That's good." My arms tingled and vibrated from the connection of ax to wood. In the woods, I was to look for twigs and branches to use as kindling. "Whenever you are in the woods or walking up from the beach, keep your eyes open for fallen branches. I never want to see you coming back to home base empty handed. We need whatever wood we can burn. If we don't have wood, we don't have fire. And if we don't have fire, we don't live."

Along with the wood, there was water. In the kitchen we had a hand pump attached to the sink, and from that I was meant to pump out the water, easy enough for just one bucket, but exhausting for many. We also had the cistern in the bathroom.

For light, we had to fill the many oil lamps and make sure their wicks were in good shape. We had to manage our candles and our batteries for the few flashlights and lanterns.

During my first days there, I didn't think there were many comforts, but as I got used to the quiet, tiring days, I learned that there were comforts in the satisfaction of knowing that you had made the fire from your own hands. You had delivered the water. You had delivered the light.

I thought of how easy it had been to flick on a light switch and turn on a tap without ever thinking about where the energy or water came from. In the summer, she said, I would help her tend the garden and can the harvest. She'd shown me the root cellar already. I'd become familiar with the rabbits in their hutches in the shed out back. She encouraged me not to get too close to them, but I'd given them names anyway. "In the summer, we'll breed some of them," she said. "You'll help with that." I hadn't told her that I might not be there come summer because, in truth, I'd stopped thinking I might leave.

At the end of the day, when we were sitting with our supper, I asked her, "Why did you choose to live like this?"

"It chose me," she said, chewing her mouthful of stew.

"But you didn't have to. No one forced you to live here. You could've left."

"Perhaps," she said, "but I didn't want to leave. Society failed me and when society fails you, there is no better place to regroup than in the woods at one's hermitage."

I thought long and hard about what she said that night, and while it didn't fully make sense to me at the time, the longer I stayed on the bluff, the more I began to feel my wounds scab over and begin to heal. Many remained fresh, and some would never heal, but some had already turned from scab to scar.

It was a school day, but the person on the sled coming to pick me up wasn't Marshall. I could tell that immediately. Even before the sled had stopped. This person was wider, shorter. I waited at the edge of the shore, unsure what to do. It was Chellie. She stopped the sled in front of me and removed her helmet. "Marshall's busy. You're stuck with me." The only reason I looked forward to going to school on these days was to see Marshall. Now he'd dumped me on Chellie. I was trapped. My mind was spinning the whole way across the lake. What could he be busy with? Why didn't he want to see me?

Once in her truck, she whistled and hummed along with the radio. Tapped her fingers on the steering wheel. "Talked to Marta," she said. "She called to make sure you were okay. Wanted me to let you know she'd been thinking of you."

"Yeah, right," I said. As if she cared about me. She could've found a way to talk to me herself if she cared so much. She could have called the school. Sent me a letter. Something. "It's her stupid job to make sure I'm okay. She doesn't really care. She's just in it for a paycheck."

"Don't shoot the messenger," Chellie said. We drove in silence for a while. I stole glances at Chellie's profile. There was something about her nose that reminded me of my mother.

"Did you know them well?" I stared straight out the windshield at the snow-covered road. Drifts pushed out onto the road near the potato field.

She looked at me. "Your folks?"

I nodded.

"Your dad was a summer kid from downstate. Didn't see him but a couple months of the year. He was up on the other side of the lake, around the bluff. I saw him fishing sometimes. Helped him with his motor once when his boat wouldn't start. Seemed like a nice guy. I was friendlier with your mother, of course. Once she met your dad, she just faded away until she was gone entirely." I wanted to ask her more questions, but there were too many pushing forward in my mouth all at once. Whenever this happened it was easier just to be quiet.

Chellie kept up the small talk as she drove me to school. I missed the silence of Marshall. He was the antithesis of me, the antithesis of West. He was popular. He was kind. He brought me back and forth to school. He played sports. He had friends. He was like Alice—like the old Alice—full of light and hope. Adored. The few times I saw him in the hallways it was like a ring of light circled him. I didn't deserve to be in the same space as him.

And yet I was.

I wanted to tell him things. I wanted him to tell me things. I wanted him to know my secrets, and I wanted to know his. I wanted to write on him like he was a yearbook and tell him just what I felt when I was with him.

Chellie drove on and my eyes drooped shut. I could hear her voice singing along with the country station on the radio, but all I saw was black. The pressure, the release.

I was in a room. A boy's room. Not one I recognized. Not West's. There were boxer shorts on the floor. Posters of basketball players on the wall.

I was the boy. I sat on the bed and bit my nails. I could feel them between my teeth. Bite, chew down, spit the nail out. It was a habit I was trying to break but couldn't. My bedroom door was shut, but I could hear their loud voices on the other side. My parents. They were arguing. As usual the argument was about me.

"There's nothing wrong with him," my mother said.

"Are you blind?" my father said. "Can't you see the boy's different? We need to find him a doctor or a priest or something."

"He doesn't need fixing," my mother said. She was always on my side. No matter what.

The man would've kept arguing but he was scared of her, my father. She was small but she didn't fight with her fists. She fought with her words. I heard a door slam, truck engine starting up, tires pulling away. He had left us again.

I stood up and walked around my room. Circled my rug. My stomach was tight and sick. I punched my fist into my hand. I couldn't be different. I was who I was. I wish he could just understand that. Out the window, snow reflected, sparkled through bare branches. I stared at the window until I saw my own reflection there. I thought, "This part of me must die. I must kill it and not let it live. I will push it down and never think of it again."

I saw my face. I was Marshall. I was in this room and I was Marshall and I was in pain, trying to kill a part of myself that I didn't want anyone to know about it. I was Marshall, and I hated myself.

I wanted to reach a hand out and touch the reflection. Tell him it would all be okay. I wanted to ask him what he had killed and why. Someday maybe I would.

Chellie shook me. "Wake up, kid," she said. She thought I was sleeping because my eyes were shut. "We're at school. I'll be back at three to pick you up."

Back at home that afternoon, I spent a lot of time thinking of Marshall, wondering why his parents fought over him. I thought of him so much until I realized that his was the first vision I'd had of a living person. So maybe it wasn't just about a person being dead, but about how I felt about a person. Maybe that is how they worked.

It was a new day. It was, in fact, the day Meme was going to show me how to use a compass. We had cleaned up the dishes, my schoolwork for the day was done, and she told me now was the time to learn about finding my direction home. We sat at the table across from each other. In her hand, she held two compasses. She handed one to me. It was smooth and felt comfortable in my hand. I turned it over and examined the back.

"Now," she began, "the first thing is to know the directions: north, south, east, and west. Do you know those?"

I rolled my eyes. "I'm not a complete idiot," I said.

"Good," she said. "Without looking at the compass, tell me which way is North."

I looked out the window, tried to remember which direction the sun rose and set. I pointed my arm in one direction. "This way," I said.

"Close," she said. "That's South, though. North is in the other direction. Marshall comes from the north to collect you. And the funny thing about this lake is that the water flows south to north. This is not normal. Now, the sun rises that way, which is east, and sets that way, which is west. Never forget that." I nodded. "This," she said holding up her compass, "is a needle compass. The red arrow points toward the magnetic north. So even if it isn't pointing to the 'N,' it is still pointing north. It is drawn to the magnetic north, just as our lake water is drawn north." I examined the face of my compass. Saw that the needle stayed in place no matter how I turned the compass. It was drawn north, toward Marshall, just as I was. Next she told me about how to use the compass, twisting it so that the black arrow in the base rested on the direction I wanted to go. "Here on the bluff, if you head south from the house, the water will always be in which direction?"

"West?" I said, unsure.

"Yes," she said. "West. So if you wander too far east, you head back west and find the shoreline. Once you've found the shoreline, you head north until you find the house. Make sense?"

"I don't know," I said, though I still wasn't sure.

"It will," she said. "When you need the compass, it will. We'll keep working on it.One thing to remember is not to hold a compass near metal when you're trying to use it. Even a staple on a map can draw the needle to it."

I put the compass on the table in front of me and spun it a few times. The red arrow kept pointing toward Marshall. "How'd you learn all of this stuff?" I asked.

"My father, mostly," she said. "He believed in self-sufficiency. Grew up in the Great Depression. Do you know about that?" I nodded. We'd learned a little bit about it in school once but I'd also watched a documentary on TV once when I was home sick and nothing else was on. It was in the 1930s just before WWII. Some rich people had lost all of their money and some people who were already poor became poorer. Some people stood in long lines for food. Others traveled far from home for work, only to find that there was none. I hadn't ever thought much about it and never realized that someone related to me had actually lived through it. "This county we're in was the poorest county in New York at that time. People were certainly hungry, but they were tough and they knew how to pull through. Those who had used the comforts of electricity and oil heat moved easily back to the old ways—to wood heat and oil lamps and candles. People already canned food each summer and fall. Some were able to keep their farms and feed their families. It was hard, it was cold, but people got through it. People like my father. Because of it, though, he never fully trusted modern conveniences. I guess I take after him." She looked out the window then. It was the most she'd ever said to me at one time and I didn't want her to stop. "I lived out in that world for a time when I was first married, but it didn't ever suit me the way living out here did. My husband, your grandfather, never could understand why I didn't want a dishwasher or central heat." She laughed. "You fall in love for stupid reasons, but you fall out of love for practical ones. Keep that in mind if you ever fall in love, young lady." She stood up, which meant it was time to get back to work. I slipped my compass in my pocket and thought of it throughout the day, the red arrow and my heart both pointing north.

The next time I had school, Marshall and I were back together again on the sled with our helmets on, racing across the lake. He couldn't hear me, so I talked on and on, telling him everything I could think to tell him. I began with the vision. The one I had seen of him. I told him that if there was something different about him, I was okay with that. I was different, too. I told him how I saw these things, people's pasts and about how it was even more than seeing.

I knew how he felt. I knew. And now I wanted him to know how I felt, too, how much I held in about myself—not just West and what he'd done, but about my mother and her past, and my grandmother, and, most importantly, how I felt about him. I kept that feeling deep inside where no one could hurt it.

"I love you," I said into the wind and hoped that instead of carrying those words away, the wind would bring them back to him. "No matter where I am, my heart points in the direction where you are." Just as we got to shore, I pushed my lips shut and quieted the rest of my words. My love for him was still secret, just as was my past secret at school.

When we were in the truck on the way to school, I waited to see if Marshall would say anything about the vision and my love for him, but as usual, he didn't speak and he hadn't heard anything I'd said, anyway. Only the wind had heard me. Once we got to the parking lot, he said, "I've got practice after school. You can take the bus and Chellie will bring you home. Or you can wait."

"I'll wait," I said, too eagerly. I would always wait.

Craig was in my same study hall. For the first few times, he sat away from me and just stared until I gave him my blank stare back. He would look away for a while and then start staring again until I gave him the blank stare again.

This day, he sat down next to me. "I've been studying your genealogy," he whispered.

"You pervert," I whispered back without looking at him. He made me anxious. I twisted my necklace around and back around my finger. I caught Craig watching me as I did it.

"I'm talking about your family tree, brainless," he said.

"Duh," I said back.

"You intrigue me." He crossed one leg over the other and bounced his foot up and down. The class monitor looked over and shushed us. Whatever.

"Do I need to file a restraining order?"

"You intrigue me," he said again. A weird thing to say once, let alone twice, but he was a weird kid. Not so unlike me, really. He and I might have been friends under different circumstances.

After a few minutes, I said. "What've you learned?" I was worried, of course, that he'd found out about West.

"Well, your father's people are not local, but your mother's are."

"So?"

"Your father's people are from Albany. Your mother grew up

on the bluff, just like you."

"And?"

"You're local. You're one of us."

"I already told you that," I said.

"What's is like living with that crazy old hermit?"

"She's not crazy," I said, though I wasn't sure. "And she's not a hermit. And she's not that old."

"What do you call living alone away from society then? Normal? Un-hermitlike?"

"I don't even know why I'm talking to you," I said and turned away.

"Your dad died young and no one knows where your mother is. Someone told me they heard you had a brother. Why isn't he here?"

"Go away," I whispered through clenched teeth. I could feel redness flowering on my cheeks, tears in my eyes.

Craig pushed away from me. "I'll find out what's going on one of these days."

I knew he would, too. It was only a matter of time. I'd gotten comfortable and started to think I might stay there. What an idiot I was. Just as I'd known before they sent me here, nowhere was safe. I needed to reach Marta. I needed her to get me out of there before everyone found out about me.

"Why don't you just mind your own business?"

"Your business is *my* business," he said. I looked down at the blank sheet of paper in front of me and focused on how many minutes there were until the end of the day.

After school, I wandered the halls, listening to the far off sounds of basketballs in the gym and cheerleaders in the foyer, practicing their inane cheers. Hey, hey, ho, ho, etc. My mind was not on them. Instead, I thought only of Craig and what he would find out next.

My phone no longer had service because no one had paid the bill. I felt stupid for not having thought of that, but I'd never had to keep track before. My mother just paid it every month. Unless she didn't have money, and then we knew well in advance that we'd be out of luck. I looked at the useless thing. I opened my contacts and wrote down a couple of the numbers in my notebook just in case, then I took off the back, removed the battery and the SD Card like I'd seen them do in the movies when they didn't want to be traced, and I dumped all of it in the trash. I immediately felt lighter. No one could reach me who I didn't want reaching me. No one could call me or text me and while that was a bit scary, it was also liberating. Maybe my grandmother was rubbing off on me. Maybe I was becoming a hermit, too.

But still, I wanted to reach out when I thought of Craig. I wanted to set up my exit plan, just in case. I remembered the old phone booth down by the front door. I headed there and entered the booth. I needed to talk to Marta. She should know. Craig was onto something and it was only a matter of time before he revealed my secret. When everyone knew the truth they would hate me. I would be the pariah again. Marshall would know. I couldn't handle the thought of him knowing about me. I pictured the look of disgust on his face. He wouldn't let me ride on his sled or in his truck anymore once he knew. Worst of all, he wouldn't let me be near him. I needed to be near him.

Inside the phone booth, generations of names and numbers had been carved into the wood. The receiver smelled stale, like old breath. I dialed the operator and told her the number I was trying to reach. "I have no money," I said. She taught me how to call collect.

When the phone rang, I waited for Marta's voice, but it rang and rang. No voicemail option. Nothing.

I tried three more times, each time more panicked than the last. Still no answer. I couldn't text. I couldn't send her an email. I was lost.

I had one more person to call. Archie. He answered on the first ring and accepted the charges.

"Laney? Are you okay? What's wrong? Did the old woman do something?" He was speaking fast. Panicked.

"It's okay, Archie. She didn't do anything."

"I've been worried about you." I rolled my eyes though he couldn't see.

"Archie, I need you to listen to me. There's a kid here—"

"What kid? What'd he do? Did anyone hurt you, Laney?" Archie's panic made me immediately uncomfortable. I didn't need him to fight this battle for me.

"Nothing," I said. "Really. It's nothing. I shouldn't have called. I'm sorry."

"Okay," he said. "But you know you can call me if you need anything. I mean it. Anything."

"Yeah," I said. "Sure. Thanks."

"I miss you, Laney," Archie said. "I miss everyone."

"I have to go now," I said and hung up. My throat felt raw and burning. Just hearing his voice brought everyone and everything back to me. That final night. West smashing down my door. I breathed deeply a few times and pushed out of the phone booth.

I wandered down the hall and found a spot in a nook near the trophy case outside the gym. There I worked on my homework until practice had been long finished. I heard voices coming down the hall toward me. I had pushed myself so far into a nook that they couldn't see me. I recognized one of the voices as Marshall's.

"She's kind of hot," the other voice said.

"Just back off," Marshall said.

"Dude, are you serious?"

"Yes," Marshall said. "Laney's a nice kid." They were talking about me. He thought I was a kid. A baby. I cringed.

"She doesn't look like a kid," the other guy said.

"Just leave her alone," Marshall said. They were past me, and I saw that Marshall pointed his finger into the other guy's chest.

"Whatever," the guy said, hands in the air. They left the building then and I waited a few minutes before I followed behind. I didn't want him to know that I overheard. I was annoyed that he thought I needed protecting, but I also remembered that the other guy thought I was hot. A junior like Marshall. No one near my age had ever called me hot before—only perverted old men like my mother's boyfriends who needed to keep their hands to themselves. They liked the extra baggage I carried, those old men. They saw my vulnerability, but to them it was something to manipulate, not bully.

When I walked out into the parking lot, Marshall was already in the truck. I got in and settled into my seat. "Sorry, I'm late," I said.

"It's cool," he said. The cab felt even more quiet than usual. I didn't mind though. I didn't even mind that I didn't get to speak to Marta. A junior guy thought I was hot. Best of all, Marshall didn't disagree.

I smiled all the way home and drew doodles in the condensation on the window. Maybe Craig wouldn't discover anything. Maybe my visions would fade away, forgotten like old dreams. Maybe I would stay here and it would all work out. Maybe.

Meme didn't wake me and the sky was already light when I woke up. I could tell by the height of the sun that it was well past when I should've been up and dressed. I pulled on the same clothes from the day before and rushed downstairs. She was sitting at the table, a bunch of photos out in front of her. Scrapbooks and journals.

"Why didn't you get me up?" I said, pulling on my boots.

"Freezing rain," she said, holding a photo up to the light and frowning.

"So?" I said.

"The kids in town don't even have school when it's freezing rain. So I figured I'd let you sleep in like they are." She smiled.

I stopped moving and listened. There was the slip-slap sound of frozen pellets against glass. I sat down at the table. If nothing else, this life had taught me to slow down and listen.

"You missed breakfast," she said. "Help yourself."

"Thanks," I said. I was hungry, so I grabbed a bowl and spoon and filled it up with granola and milk from the propane fridge. I sat down at the table and craned my neck to see the photos. Most were black and white, but not all. Some Polaroids and snapshots with zig-zaggy edges.

"Be careful not to spill on these," she said. She patted the books like they were small children.

"What is it?" I asked.

"My memories," she said, looking at me. "You have good eyesight?" I nodded. "You can help then, but not until after you've eaten and washed your hands."

Once I'd cleaned up, I sat back down with her and she handed me a stack of photos. She explained that some had names and dates written on the back—those I should put in a special pile.

It didn't take long before I stumbled over some photos of my mom as a baby. I had never thought much about babies. Was never interested in babysitting the way some girls my age were. But the picture of my mother as a baby moved me.

She was a baby in a tub, smiling with two small bottom teeth. A hand steadied her from behind, a woman's hand. It must have been Meme's. She saw what I was looking at. "That's your mom, but you probably already knew that," she said.

I hoped to find more pictures of her, but instead the photos I had were older and faded—groups of young women and young men. A pretty young woman with black hair, Meme, dressed in fishing waders. There she was on the beach in a black strapless bathing suit, looking glamorous and striking a pose. I longed to ask her about these photos but we were still not fully comfortable with each other. Not that I had ever been comfortable with anyone. Except maybe West, but only when we were younger. We used to play together. I remember that. We had fun.

But he changed when he was about my age. Stopped being nice to me. Stopped coming into my room at night and making plans for the future. He would graduate and go to college, he said, and I could live with him in his dorm. We would both get out at the same time. But then he met Mark and stopped even looking at me, like I wasn't there in front of him anymore. The only way he would speak to Alice was to yell, and he never talked to Archie. When Archie tried to discipline him, he'd just say, "One day I'll kill you all in your sleep. Just wait." Then he'd mimic slitting his throat.

That's when I started locking my door at night. If I heard him awake and moving around, I would avoid leaving my room. He stopped going to school on a regular basis. Alice threatened to kick him out. "Do it," he said. "I dare you." Instead she broke down crying and begging him. Telling him over and over again how much she loved him. "You're my baby, West," she said.

West rolled his eyes and said, "Whatever."

I remembered that in one of Alice's albums, she had an almost identical photo of West in a bathtub. Smiling, tiny teeth, fat fists raised in pleasure, waving at the world. *Look at me. I exist.*

I don't know how someone goes from being a smiling baby to a boy who kills people for fun. I wanted someone to tell me how that happened. I looked at Meme. Her eyes were focused on the photo in front of her. She would not be able to tell me. She didn't ever really know West. Not the West he'd become anyway. She knew the baby.

She picked up the photo of my mom in the bathtub again and held it up so I could see, "Look," she said. "It's a picture of my grandson, West." I thought she was making a horrible joke, but when I looked at her eyes I saw that she was being serious.

I felt scared then. Her eyes were watery, unfocused.

"Are you okay, Meme?" I asked.

"Of course, Mary," she said. "Why are you always asking me that?"

"Who's Mary?" I asked. Did she see someone? A ghost? I turned around.

"You," she said, a bit less sure of herself. "My sister." She put her hands to her eyes for a second and then said, "You better go put some wood on the fire." I left her then to do my chore.

After I put some logs on the fire, I knelt there and stared at the embers, heard their crackling. It was happening again, the vision. Blackness into nothing into light.

My hands, my mother's hands, were washing in water, splashing. I was washing a baby, a boy. Singing to him, "My Bonnie Lies over the Ocean." He cooed and smiled and splashed his fat hands into the warm suds. "My baby," I said. "I could not love you more." And I felt in every part of my body the most enormous, all-encompassing love. There was nothing to compare it to. It was like how I felt for my mother when I loved her so, but more than that. This baby was me or some part of me.

The baby switched then as did my hands. I had gone from my mother and West to my grandmother and my mother. Nearly the same scene, but different. What was the same was the feeling of mother for child. The love didn't only please me, it hurt me. I wanted to protect the baby.

As I wiped a tiny washcloth over my baby's body, I said, "You're my favorite person," in my grandmother's voice and I felt that. I felt how you could unequivocally say to your child that you loved them above all else and mean it. Truly mean it.

I stared deep into the fire and wondered about my grandmother and my mother, about my mother and West. About my mother and me. I wondered if she had loved me that deeply. I wondered, too, if that love would carry on even now, after she had died. At some point I'd stopped believing that she loved but maybe she had after all. Maybe she even still did.

Later in the day when we ate together, Meme seemed back to normal. Her eyes looked clear and she had color in her cheeks. Maybe she had just been tired. Maybe her eyes had played tricks on her. The winter light wasn't strong and she was getting older. She was fine. I stopped asking her if she was okay and believed that she was.

Then I realized that she'd started to mean something to me. If I worried about her, didn't that mean that maybe I cared about her? Maybe just a little?

She caught me staring at her and snapped, "What?"

Yes, she was back to her old self. "Nothing," I said. I kept that feeling tight inside as I had learned to do.

Seven

The afternoon sun was hanging on just a bit longer each day. I wasn't sure what would happen come spring, how I would get to school and whether that meant I would no longer spend time with Marshall. I wanted to be with him every minute, every second. Not once in the weeks since I'd known him had I felt anything other than joyful in his presence. One afternoon when he dropped me off at the beach, Marshall lingered. He wanted to tell me something. I waited, excited. "There's a game on Friday night," he said. "You can come if your grandmother doesn't mind you being out late."

"She won't mind," I said, not knowing if that was true. We arranged a time for him to pick me up. "I can't wait to see you play," I said and immediately regretted it, but he already had his visor down and was headed back across the lake. It didn't matter that I hated basketball and sports in general. Especially now. Especially after what had happened. After what my brother had done. Craig had stopped picking at me, but had not stopped staring at me. Every week when I went to school, I saw him, always nearby, his gears turning.

But Craig didn't matter. Only Marshall did. Maybe I could learn to love basketball. The most important thing was that Marshall asked me. I wasn't sure if he was being friendly, or if this was a date. I knew he was with my distant-cousin Linda, but maybe he really liked me. There was no one to ask for a second opinion. I'd never had a close friend like that. We'd moved around too much, and when we'd finally settled at our last home, I was already beyond the point where I was friend material for anyone. West and I were already established as the school freaks. The difference between us was that I went inward and stewed unhappily on my lot in life. I also reached out to other worlds through the books I read and through the company I found in the woods. I also found comfort in the future, telling myself over and over again that when I graduated and made my way out into the world, everyone would regret not having known me in high school. They would regret having discounted me. I would be famous and beautiful. I would be wanted. I wrapped myself in these fantasies and they gave me great comfort, whereas West chose another path. His fantasies were dark and filled with anger. His fantasies consumed him and fed his desire for retribution. And then his fantasies became reality.

I walked up the path slowly, pushing away thoughts of West. I wanted to linger in the moment of Marshall asking me to go to his game. How had his face looked? Was there an inflection in his voice? I could've lived in that moment forever.

When I thought of what it would actually be like to be alone with him in his truck at night, I freaked out. I had no idea what I would say, or what he would say. It would either be the best thing ever or the absolute worst. I had no ability to see the future. I could only see the crumbled past as it slipped away into nothing.

"Today, I am going to teach you how to forage," Meme said. "You won't put this lesson into action until spring, really, but it's never too early to start learning about wild edibles and mycology." As soon as she began, I zoned out. It was like she was speaking a foreign language. So boring. So confusing.

"Pay attention," she said loudly, rapping her knuckles in front of me on the table. "This is serious. If you make a mistake with what you pick and put in your mouth, it could be the last mistake you ever make." I sat up straight. "Many wild edibles and mushrooms are perfectly harmless, but some are not so harmless. Some will kill you quick. So keep your eyes open and your mind focused. Got it?" I nodded. She handed me a field guide. "This is your guide. Study it and learn it well. We'll start with fiddleheads in the spring and move on from there to mushrooms, leeks, berries, nuts. Questions?"

"Why do we need to eat this stuff if we have food from our garden? I mean, isn't it a lot of work and sort of dangerous? What if I pick the wrong thing?"

She sighed. "We eat it because it is part of our environment. It is local to us. It fights the same bacteria, viruses, and molds that we fight. Eating these foods will help to build up our immunity, thus keeping us away from needing modern medicine. I don't much like visiting the doctor, do you?" I shook my head. "Good," she said, "Then we're in agreement. Any other questions?" I shook my head again. "The most important thing I want you to think of is about how, when we forage, we must respect nature. If we respect her, she will continue to provide for us. So that means not leaving a mess and not taking more than we need. Got it?" I nodded.

She left me with the book and I glanced through the pages. Mushrooms growing in dark, green places. Sun cutting through the high branches. One photo of a fiddlehead pushing up from beneath a compost of leaves, bright green and delicate. I was touched by its strength and lost in how the light illuminated it. The fiddlehead had pushed up through the darkness and lived. Despite being covered over and forgotten through the long, cold winter, it had beaten the odds and survived.

On Friday afternoon, I told Meme that I was going to the game with Marshall.

"He's bringing me," I said. I didn't even ask her.

"I don't think it's a wise idea," she said, staring right into my eyes. I wouldn't look away. "Is this about a boy?" she asked.

"No," I said, trying to push emotion from my face. She stared hard at me.

"Better not be."

"It's not," I said. Her eyes were crawling all over my head, looking for a way in.

For a minute that seemed to last forever, she was silent. "Don't be late getting home or I'll send the troopers out to look for you," she said. I didn't bother to ask her how she'd get in touch with the troopers, seeing as we had no phone. I was too happy that she was going to let me go to say much of anything, other than to thank her over and over again until she told me to quiet down and set the table.

After dinner, she had me scrubbing so many pots that I worried I didn't have time to do much more than brush my teeth and wash my face before I had to go down to the beach and wait for Marshall. He'd told me he'd be on the beach to get me by six on Friday. The game started at seven-thirty.

I'd never been on a date before, but this was what it must feel like—all of this nervous anticipation. I thought maybe I wanted to feel close to someone, but I also wasn't sure because there was something scary about being close to someone, as well. It would've been nice to have someone hold me and tell me it was okay. I couldn't remember the last time someone had actually touched me. Held my hand. Pushed my hair back from my face. I thought of my mother's face then. Her hands reaching out to me. I shook my head and pushed her away. Marshall would probably think I was a freak if I said any of that to him.

I wanted to be like Linda. It seemed like everything came easy to her. Her prettiness didn't come from her making herself pretty. It was just there. I'd watched her in the hall. She flirted with all of the boys, whether they were attractive or not. They watched her. All of them.

I was not that type of girl. I was sure no one could even see me half the time. People bumped into me. People looked through me. People started talking before I'd finished my sentence. I wanted to yell, I am here, but I was afraid no one would hear even that.

I AM HERE.

As usual, our trip to town was silent. When we got to school, Marshall left me to get ready for the game. I paid for a ticket and found a spot in the gym. I was one of the first spectators on the bleachers. Linda and the other cheerleaders were there already, practicing. I'd never been to a game before, not even back home. The whole idea would've been funny to me then, all the popular kids would be there and I would've been both hating them and wishing they wanted me with them. Instead, I'd watched movies on television with basketball games and cheerleaders and huge crowds. I expected excited anticipation, but instead felt a sense of dread that I couldn't quite put my finger on.

When the cheerleaders took a break from warming up, Linda came over to where I was sitting. She was smiling, so she must not be angry that Marshall had brought me, if she even knew. She gave one of her little waves. "Glad you could make it, Laney," she said, sitting down next to me and drinking from a water bottle. "Marshall said he was going to give you a ride here. He's good that way." And so that's all it was, according to her. A ride. I tried not to let my disappointment show. I didn't want to give her the satisfaction, if that's what she wanted. "Maybe you can hang out with us for a while afterward?"

"Maybe," I said, but it came out in a whiny way that made me ashamed.

"I better get back to the squad." She bounded down the bleachers and left me by myself, defeated. I was nothing but the third wheel. I wanted to leave right then but didn't know how to get back. There were no buses home. No taxis. I couldn't call Meme and get a ride from her. I was mortified that I'd thought this whole thing was something more than Marshall being nice to me. I was sure that everyone could see my mistake and that they all were laughing about it.

I wanted out.

The bleachers started filling up. People. Mothers and fathers and kids. Teachers I recognized. Classmates. My hands hurt and it took me a second to realize that they hurt because I was crushing them together. My brain flashed white and then the air around me splotched with bright lights. I was in a gym. There was a basketball game about to begin. I heard a bang and jumped in my seat. It was only the sound of a basketball hitting the floor.

Bang, bang, bang, bang. More balls.

I clutched at the neck of my sweater and pulled it away from my skin.

Bang, bang, bang.

I looked out to the floor and saw only players and basektballs. Marshall was on the court, bouncing a ball, staring at me. Actually looking at and seeing me. "Are you okay?" he mouthed. I tried to smile, but felt too shaky and sweaty. I looked around and saw that Linda had watched this interaction. She looked weird—pissed, or maybe concerned. I wasn't sure. Craig was across the gym from me with a camera. He focused it in my direction and started taking photos. His camera flashed and flashed and flashed at me. I covered my face with my hands, my hair, and bent forward. I twisted my necklace around and back. Around and back. But it didn't work to soothe me. My breathing quickened. I felt feverish. I put my hand on my forehead the way I remembered my mother doing when I was little and sick. My head felt cool and clammy. I couldn't breathe.

I needed to get out of there. Something horrible was about to happen. Something really bad was going to happen. People were going to die. I had to let them know. I turned from side to side, looking for an escape. People filed in through the gym doors. I saw Linda watching me still and waving. I didn't wave back.

Then I saw Linda signaling someone over to me—Mrs. Ringly, the guidance counselor. Linda said something to her and pointed to me. The last thing I remembered was Mrs. Ringly jogging toward me, just before I blacked out.

What none of them realized is that I didn't lose consciousness entirely. I was in deep. My body taken over by the worst, most overwhelming vision yet.

I was crouching behind a brick wall. A bus idled nearby. My heart was beating so fast that I felt I might faint for real. Someone was behind me, breathing hard. I knew not to turn around. My job was to keep my eyes on the parking lot.

It was my old school. The bus, one of ours. It was packed and I could hear voices from inside it all the way over to where I was. "Okay," the person behind me said. I recognized the voice. It was Mark. "Now," he said and pushed me from behind. I wanted to hesitate. "Move," he said. I wanted to turn back, but I couldn't. I moved forward. We ran across the parking lot. Mark was laughing and I laughed, too, because I could not stop myself from laughing. I didn't want to stop myself.

"This is it," he yelled and reached a hand over for a high five. "Are you ready?"

"Hells to the yeah," I said and slapped his hand. He ran up the bus steps in front of me. I stopped at the bottom step for just a second. I looked back over my shoulder. I could've run back. Instead, I stepped up and followed him. I wasn't scared to die. I wasn't scared of anything. This was it. We were going to do it. We were finally going to do it. They would all know now. They would know how we felt. They would know the fear and the anger and the hatred. They would know how powerful we were. They would know that they should've paid attention to us. That they should've been nice to us. They would know it all.

And then I would be released. I would be free.

I woke up on a lumpy cot in the coach's office in the girls' locker room. Mrs. Ringly was there and someone who must have been a nurse or a doctor. She was taking my pulse. I tried to sit up. "Is everyone okay?"

"Whoa," Mrs. Ringly said. "Lie back down for a minute, sweetie." She brought me juice and a cookie, like when you give blood.

Blood. I saw it everywhere. My heart started to bang again. The nurse guided my head back to the pillow and put a cold cloth on it. "Just breathe," she said.

When I was calmer and the nurse asked me a bunch of questions about panic attacks and how long I'd had them.

"Am I dying?" I asked. I held up my arms and examined them for blood and cuts.

"No," she said. "You're fine. Your heart is strong. It's your head that made you feel sick." She patted my hand. I heard the sounds of the basketball game through the walls. The cheering. The silence. The buzzers. It must have been halftime because we heard the away team in the locker room. Everything was okay. Everyone was okay. No one got hurt. No one but me.

"Is there someone I can call to pick you up?" Mrs. Ringly asked. I shook my head. There was no one. I didn't want to see Marshall after passing out. I was too embarrassed and so I agreed to let her give me a ride home.

After halftime we left the locker room. Mrs. Ringly seemed to know that I'd rather die than see anyone. During the ride, she gave up asking me questions about what happened. Instead, she told me a bunch of propaganda, all of the great things about our school. How kids all knew each other's names and how there was very little bullying. She talked about all of the opportunities for scholarships at graduation. She talked about school pride. She talked about how it was okay to be different and how if I ever needed someone to talk to, I knew where to find her.

I stopped listening. All I could think about was what happened to me in the gym. I was sure I was going to die. I was sure everyone was going to die. It didn't make sense, though, because West and Mark were dead and they weren't coming back. I wanted to call Marta and ask her if it was true that West was really dead. I hadn't seen his body, after all. No one would let me. They wheeled him out in a body bag. I saw the trolley moving through our family room in slow motion. The covering seemed to glow with his body within it, like a cocoon.

The next time I saw him, he was just ashes in a box. So I had no way to know for sure if he was really dead.

Maybe he had escaped. Maybe he had followed me and was up here, haunting these woods, waiting for his chance to get the rest of us, to get me.

He had wanted me to die. He died trying to get in my room. He died trying to kill me.

Mrs. Ringly dropped me off at Chellie's as I'd asked her to. I waved goodbye to her from the porch and knocked on the door. I waited for a few minutes and then knocked again. If she wasn't there, I was going to have to walk across the lake by myself in the dark. I didn't want to cross over alone. I knocked and knocked and finally Chellie came to the door, looking disheveled and wrapped in a blanket. Her nose was red and her hair was all messed up on one side.

"Come in, come in," she said, opening her door. "I've got germs though, so don't get too close."

"I don't want to bother you," I said. "Can I borrow a flashlight?"

"You're going to walk over?" she asked, coughing.

"Yes," I said.

"Ever done it before?"

"No," I said.

"Do you want me to bring you?" She was shivering beneath

her blanket. Probably a fever.

"I can do it myself," I said. She watched me for a bit and then retrieved a flashlight. She found one, but the batteries were dead, so she hunted through her kitchen cabinets for some fresh ones. Then I noticed her phone.

"Can I use your phone?" I asked. "I need to make a call."

"Sure, kid," she said. "No problem." She handed me the flashlight and batteries. "I'm just going to go lie down."

"I'll call collect," I said.

She swatted her hand in the air. "Nah," she said. "Just call."

Once she was in her room, I picked up the phone and dialed Marta's number, which I'd memorized. It rang five times. I hung up and called again. It rang and rang. I pictured a darkened room where the phone sat. The kitchen with the ticking fridge and dripping faucet. Moonlight falling through the window by the sink.

I could not reach her. She might've simply been out, but my gut was telling me that something was wrong. I felt that she was not okay. I needed to hear her voice and for her to hear mine. I needed to know she was okay.

I picked up the phone to dial again, hesitated with my hand over the keypad. I punched in a different number. One I had memorized long ago when I was younger and afraid. My old neighbor answered on the second ring. "Hello?"

"Mrs. Coughlin?" She'd taught me her phone number when we first met and told me to use it anytime I needed help. She had said, "But make sure you're calling because it's an emergency and no one else is there to help you." She didn't want to be seen by Alice as butting into our business. She would help us, but only up to a point.

"Yes, that's me. Have you forgotten my voice so quickly Laney Kates?"

"No," I said.

"I trust you're not calling to just say hello seeing as you've not so much as sent me a postcard since you've been gone."

"It's an emergency," I said. "I need your help."

"What's wrong?" Her voice was all business again. I pictured her standing in her kitchen, talking into her old-fashioned wall phone, gazing out the window, eyes seeking the ever-present squirrels.

"I can't get in touch with my…Marta. The woman from social services? Can you please help me find her? I need to talk to her? Please."

"I don't know the woman, Laney Kates." She was getting tired of me now, as she usually did.

"Her phone just rings and rings," I said. "I have her address. She gave it to me."

"I see. So, you want me to put my boots and jacket on and drive over there right now?" I didn't say anything. "It's cold out, Laney."

"Please."

She sighed. I knew I was winning her over. "And tell her what exactly?"

"Tell her I need help," I said.

"Do you want to be more specific?" she sounded concerned now.

"No," I said. I read the address to her and she promised she was writing it down.

"Is that all?"

"Yes, that's all. Thank you."

"You take care, Laney," she said and hung up before I could say anything else. I pictured her now, slipping on her boots and crunching across the snow to her old car. She would drive to Marta's house. She would knock. She would find her. And then what? I wasn't sure.

I had a dollar in my pocket, which I left by the phone for Chellie with a note that said thanks and that I would return the flashlight. Quietly, I let myself out and walked down to the shore. I remembered something my mother told me about only using a flashlight if you really needed to. "It's better to let your eyes get used to the dark," she said. We'd been out in our backyard at night during the summer. There was supposed to be a meteor shower. She woke me up so that we could see it together. We sat wrapped in blankets, watching and waiting. I fell asleep leaning against her, but she nudged me awake. "When we die, I want us all to come back as a meteors," she said.

I was pretty sure she would not get that wish.

I was pretty sure people like West who killed other people came back again as people who killed other people. The cycle goes around and around.

I took one tentative step out onto the ice and then another. I followed the rutted tracks of the sleds. I will be okay, I said to myself. Over and over: I will be okay.

I could see the bluff in the distance, lit by the celestial sky. I didn't need a flashlight. I could see everything—every outline and nuance as if it were the bright of day. There were places of light and of shade. The moon glowed coolly above.

I wanted to believe I was safe living on the bluff with Meme and going to school with Marshall but everything felt as unsure and as tenuous as the ice beneath my feet.

I felt West's victims surround me. They were helping me forward. They guided my feet. I was nearly halfway across when I stopped and looked up again. Everything was still. No wind. Above the sky was awash with undulating color. I reached a hand up to touch, but found only air. These were the spirits of West's victims. I was not scared. I opened my arms to them. "I'm sorry," I shouted up to the sky. I lay down in that spot and looked up at them.

I should've done something.

I should've done something, but I didn't know what he would do.

I thought he wanted to kill me.

I would die there and join them. Perhaps that was the best answer: to let everything go and die right there and become one of them, become one of West's victims. I was one already, after all.

I heard the sound of a sled farther off and then closer. I struggled to stand up. The lights were shining in my eyes. He had come for me. I started to run, my feet breaking through snow, hunted. I ran until I fell, and then I began to crawl. I would not let him find me. Not like this. Not now.

I was like one of the animals I'd learned to track. Prey. Though my intention was never to harm them, just to learn about them. I didn't know his intention, and I didn't want to know. I only wanted away. I moved forward, the beach in sight. I might make it to the trees before he found me.

I might make it.

Eight

Marshall stopped his sled, took off his helmet and walked to where I was crawling. I stopped moving and hung my head, moved into a sitting position and cradled my face in my gloves. I was consumed by shame. I held my breath and waited for him to say something. "Are you all right?" The cold was alive and breathing with us, though it did not stand between us.

"Do you see them?" I wanted to not be alone in sharing this moment with the victims. I pointed upward. There they were—an outward manifestation of my visions. All around us the sky was lit by color, the blood of the victims. If he didn't see them, then I would know for sure that I'd lost my mind.

"Yes," he said.

"So I'm not crazy?" I said. "You really see them?"

"Aurora borealis," he said.

"What?" I looked up at him.

"The northern lights," he said. The lights in the sky were real, but they weren't my ghosts. They were the colored lights that filled the northern sky a few times throughout the year. I'd read about them, but some things must be experienced.

"I thought they were ghosts," I said.

"Some people think they are spirits," he said, taking a step closer to me. "It's not such a crazy thought."

I remembered his game. "Did you win?"

"Yes, but what happened to you?"

"Low blood sugar," I said quickly. "I should always carry a snack." I stood up to show I was okay. The visions were getting more powerful. They were taking over my body. I was becoming West, becoming my mother. Marshall would never understand that. No one would.

"You looked like you were dead and then I couldn't find you. Mrs. Ringly told me she gave you a ride. I knew you'd be walking out here by yourself like this. I left as soon as I could." These words were the most he had ever said to me.

But then I remembered that I was a third-wheel to him. That Linda was his girl. He didn't want me. He especially wouldn't want me if he knew why I'd been sent to the Adirondacks in the first place. I was tainted.

"I'm fine," I said. I held up my hands and patted my arms. "See? I'm not dead. You don't have to worry. I can take care of myself, like always." I turned from him and kept walking.

"Laney," he said, catching up to me, catching my arm. He turned me around. He was touching me. It was happening.

"What?" I tilted my chin up to look straight into his eyes as if they would tell me the truth. Instead, I could see the sky reflected— the lights moved across his pupils.

"I was scared you were hurt," he said. "I care about you."

"No," I said, "You can't."

"Why not?" he said.

"Because," I said. All my life I'd waited for someone like Marshall to say these things to me. All my life I'd waited for someone to love me.

"You're special," he said. I fought the urge to roll my eyes, to push it all away. To push him away like I did everything else wonderful and fragile and dear.

"I'm not anything," I said.

"You are special. I can see that you are. I know that you are," he said. He pulled me in closer to him. "I know you need help, but I don't know how to help you," he said. "I'm sorry." I wasn't sure what to do, so I let him hold me tight. The skin of his face was warm against my cheek and his breath smelled like Bazooka gum, not something I thought anyone other than small children chewed. "I know how it feels to be scared," he said. "I know how it feels to not belong." The piece of himself that he'd killed. He was talking about that. I wanted to ask him about it, but the time was not right. Not then.

The sky wrapped around us, pulling us tighter together.

West whispered to me, "A gift before I take you with me."

I didn't want to worry about him anymore. I wanted him to go away for good, but he was there now hanging above us, marring this otherwise treasured moment.

Anything could be taken away from me.

When we moved away from each other, Marshall said, "You must be freezing." I was cold but I didn't want to leave. I wanted to stay with him always. I wanted to live in his arms and for him to live in mine. Soon I would be sixteen and I finally knew what it meant to be in love for real and not just from a book.

He brought me to the sled and got me settled and then we headed to my home. He left me at the beach with another hug. "Take care of yourself," he said. "We'll talk more the next time I see you." Everything was almost perfect except that I couldn't let Meme find out about Marshall and I couldn't let Marshall find out about West.

A boy I liked had touched me in a gentle way. All of my touches before this had been dares and challenges. Pushes and pulls. Never with anyone I actually had feelings for. These feelings.

These feelings would engulf me. These feelings would blanket me. These feelings would kill me if I let them. These feelings were assassins. There was not one thing in this world that wasn't deadly and these feelings might've been the deadliest.

I would need to find a way to control them and not let them consume me, the way my mother had. She let the love she had for the man in her life eventually rule her. I didn't want to be like her, but I felt myself slipping into the belief that if only he loved me as much as I loved him, then nothing and no one else would matter.

As I lay in bed, still shivering from the cold after lying to Meme about what a fun night it had been, I went over the scene from the middle of the frozen lake in my mind. He'd pulled me close. He'd chosen to do that. Chosen me. He said he was scared, too. It was what would bind us together, our fear. Just as fear had once bound West and me. Fear might not have been the best connection. Fear led to anger. Fear led to death. Fear also created adrenalin, which helped us to survive.

But there was something else between us, too. I felt it. I know he must have, as well. There was love. There was. And once there was love, it was hard to feel anything else. I shut my eyes and the pressure began, pushing down on me. I didn't want it. Not then.

I was on the sled by myself. It was night. This night. The lights were all around me in the sky. I clenched my teeth and drove back toward home. I didn't want to go there, alone, and face my father's disapproval, if he was even there. I would tell him we won the game but even that would not be enough to wipe away the shame he felt about me. I would never be good enough for him. Not anymore. Never again. Never.

I got home and put away my sled. My father's truck was there, the engine still ticking, the hood warm. He'd just gotten home from a night at the bar. I walked slowly up to the front stoop. The porch light was lit.

I climbed the steps, took a deep breath, and entered the house. He was at the table waiting for me, a beer in his hand. "You're daughter's home," he yelled back to my mother who was in the other room watching one of her shows. He stared right at me and smiled, then he laughed. I wasn't sure whether to turn around and head back out or push through. He stopped laughing and stared hard at me.

I pushed through back to my bedroom. It didn't bother me that he made fun of me. What bothered me was that he hated me so much. He looked at me like I was dirt.

I stood in front of the mirror and looked at my face, the one everyone thought was so beautiful and perfect. What I saw was ugliness.

My heart filled with regret. I should have told Laney tonight. I know she would understand. I know it.

Back in my bed, I shivered again. I had seen Marshall and he was in pain. I wanted to take his pain and wrap it around me. Why did his father not approve of him? I couldn't imagine that he had done anything to deserve such hatred. He was all that was good and beautiful in the world. He was filled with light. He was love.

I needed to let him know that I would always be there for him. I made that one promise to myself and I would keep it. I would not let one more thing go unsaid. I had let West slip away and he had done something unspeakable. I would not let Marshall slip away.

It was Saturday morning and I was in the bathroom brushing my hair. I wondered if I looked different to Meme now that I was in love. I smiled at myself. He said I was special. He meant it in a good way.

No one had ever thought that about me before, not even Alice. It was understood that West was her special one, while I was the quiet one who didn't cause trouble. I stayed in the shadows, not wanting to be seen.

I was seen now.

I remembered the phone call I'd made and what I'd asked of Mrs. Coughlin, and I wished I could take it back. She would've spoken to Marta by now. I was going to have to call her again and let her know everything was okay. I panicked momentarily, thinking she would be on her way to get me, but then realized that the chances of that were slim. It was a weekend. Everything was okay.

I was staying. Nothing could get to me anymore. Even Meme was growing on me. This bluff was my home.

When I left the bathroom, Meme enlisted me once again to separate photos. I found one of my parents together. They looked so young, like my age almost. My mother's hair was shorter in the picture and she was a bit heavier but still pretty. And my dad was tall and big and dark. I flipped it over and read the date. I counted back the years and months. She was pregnant with West in the photo.

Meme looked up from her work and grabbed the photo from me. "What've you got there?" She examined it, looked at me over her glasses. "Hmmm," she said. "Don't figure you know much about your father do you?" I shook my head. "He ended up going into the service not long after this photo was taken. They'd just gotten back together. He, uh…I don't know how to sugar-coat this other than to just say it. He didn't want to have a baby. Thought they were too young, which was about the smartest thing he ever thought. He broke up with her. Broke her heart, but then she convinced him they could do it and so he agreed. Your mom was supposed to go to college." She sighed, put the picture down on the table. "But it wasn't meant to be."

"Couldn't she have gone to college anyway?"

"She had responsibilities." Meme looked right at me in a way that was almost blaming. "Wasn't too long after she had West that you came along."

"What happened to my dad?" I hoped that finally I would get the real answer. The truth.

"She killed him," Meme said without hesitation.

"What?" I said. "Who killed him?"

"Your mother," she said. My heart stopped beating and my

body covered over in ice.

"It's not true," I said. "She loved him."

"You may not want to believe it, but it's true."

"You're crazy," I said. I stood up quickly and my chair toppled, surprising both of us as it clattered to the floor.

"Believe what you want to believe, but I know the truth. Love kills you." She leaned back against her chair and folded her arms across her chest. I couldn't believe that I'd thought I could love her. She was horrible. Just like the rest of them. Just like West. I raced upstairs and found the comfort of my bed, the blanket over my head. She was punishing me for my night out. She could see the love on me. She wanted to kill it. No wonder my mother had left.

I wished I could've found the road out of there—that road led to freedom and to Marshall. I wished he wasn't across the lake—the wind whipped cold drifts across the widest part of it that day. With the wind chill it was forty below. I wouldn't have lasted long out there.

I longed for my mother's voice. For some touch of home. I reached for my backpack and snaked it up under the covers with me. I opened West's book and, using the flashlight, I read:

Mark said that we should get rid of our families first. He said that killing them would be the nicest thing we could do. "Do you want them to live in such a screwed up world?"

I can't argue with him but I'm not sure I can kill them. I've tried a practice run before—stood outside Laney's door at night and listened with my ear through the hollow wood. I can almost make out her breathing. She always locks her door now but she has no idea how easy it is for me to open it. I use a paperclip to slowly open the lock and then I am in, standing over her bed as she sleeps. She doesn't even know I'm there and it'd be so easy to put a pillow over her head and then shoot a few times into the pillow. It wouldn't even be like killing her. It'd be like saying good night to her and see you soon in paradise. It'd be like saying, you'll thank me for this later.

I tell Mark I'll think about killing my family. I tell him I'm 95% sure I'll do it.

I held the pillow up to my mouth to muffle the cry that came out against my will. I lay there thinking of West in my room in the dark and soon the vision came, strong and fast, like a bolt of electricity running through me.

It was dark but I knew my way around the room. I had been in there hundreds of times before. I knew where her book bag was hooked over the chair. I knew where she dropped her pile of clothes each night. I knew this room. I had the hunting knife in my pocket. It was ready.

She moved in her sleep and I froze. I made up a lie I'd tell her if she woke up. I'd say that I wanted to borrow a book. She has so many stupid books and doesn't realize that there is nothing important to learn in her stupid stories. She needs to read some philosophy. She needs to read some manifestos. She doesn't need to read about killing mockingbirds and stuff like that.

She settled back into sleep and I moved forward.

She was on her back, face turned up to the ceiling. One hand curled up near her face. She was my sister. I hated her and I loved her, or I used to love her. She didn't even seem human to me anymore. No one did. No one felt what Mark and I felt. We were as close as two people could be. He knew how I felt and I know how he felt. No one else mattered. Not even our families. Especially not our families.

I was so close that I could hear her breathing. I held the knife tight in my sweating hand, pulled it out. I opened the blade quietly. I knew this knife almost as well as I knew her. I brought it closer to her skin, her throat. I felt her breath on my wrist. I saw the beat of her artery in her neck. Her hand. I remembered holding it as a child. We'd been small once. Small together. But now we were grown and apart.

Her breath was hot again on the hair of my wrist. I felt sick. I would throw up soon. I backed away, covered my mouth, pushed the vomit back in. I left her room, shutting the door behind me.

I sat up. My breath was coming fast, my heart pounding. There I had been sleeping with no idea how close I was to being dead. The only comfort I was left with was that he decided not to kill me. It would've been better if he hadn't stopped himself. I thought with relief of him plunging a knife into my heart. I would've died quickly and with ease, instead of lingering and dying slowly with guilt and shame.

The rest of the day passed in an angry blur. I'd awoken so happy in the morning only to have all of my happiness ruined. I slept little that night, hoping no more visions would come. Each one now was stronger, more potent. I felt as if I was becoming all of these others whose lives I saw and lived. Fully becoming them. I didn't want to be West. Ever.

I spent the rest of the weekend barely speaking to Meme. If I had to live with her, I would live with her, but it didn't mean I had to like her. I'd lived with plenty of people I hadn't liked. Archie, for example.

I was there now for Marshall. For him alone.

On Monday morning, Marshall and I were awkward with each other, or maybe it just seemed that way to me. I kept hoping he would touch me again, but then when we got to school and I slid across the seat to him. Marshall put his hand on the door. He looked anxious. I guessed he might be worried about Linda finding out. He smiled before he left the truck. I wanted to reassure him about what I'd seen, about his father and his father's cruelty, but I couldn't find the right words. To reveal to him my visions so soon might unravel all that we'd strung together.

In homeroom, Craig perched on my desk before the bell rang, hovering and crowding my space. I wanted to push him away. "What happened to you on Friday?" He looked right into my eyes and would not look away.

"Low blood sugar," I said. "I fainted."

"Yeah, yeah. That's the party line, but I'm not buying it," he said.

"Don't care if you're buying it," I said.

"What's going on with you and Marshall?" I was surprised he didn't have a microphone in his hand and a camera ready to film me.

"Nothing," I said, though I smiled at his insinuation.

"You were sitting very close to him in his truck this morning."

I stared him down with all of the hatred I could muster.

He held his hands up in defeat and stood up. "Hey," he said. "Easy. I'm just doing my job."

Later, I saw Marshall and Linda in the hall together. She looked upset and he was comforting her. He probably told her about us. He didn't look happy.

He turned his head from her and saw me. She looked up and saw me, too, and noticed that he was looking at me. In that moment, I saw her wheels turning. She figured out that we were together. She turned around and slammed her locker shut. She turned and started in my direction. I backed up. "Laney, wait," she said. "I have to talk to you."

"I'm going to be late for class," I said and sprinted away from her. I didn't care what she had to say. All that mattered was Marshall. It seemed he broke up with her and so there were no more obstacles. Everything was working out. Nothing ever worked out for me like that. Marshall was the answer to all of my problems. Once I had him, everything else would go away and I would be reborn, all of my sins and the sins of my family washed away. If beautiful, perfect Marshall wanted me, then everyone would have to accept me as I was.

•

Last period and I headed to my locker to get my jacket. There were a group of kids standing around nearby. Some of them were laughing and some were covering their mouths. I knew where it came from. Craig was there, talking, showing them something on his tablet.

I froze. I couldn't move forward and I couldn't go backward. Then Craig spotted me and got in my face again. "I posted a piece about you and Marshall," he said. So that was it. Maybe Linda had read it.

"Good for you," I said. I tried to sound nonchalant but I was secretly pleased. He had helped me more than he knew. He kept staring at me, smirking. I twisted my necklace back and around my finger. He was making me nervous.

"That's a beautiful necklace," he said. "I've noticed you enjoy fondling it so much." *Fondling* was such a gross word. I frowned. "I got to thinking about it last night because I was watching some footage of the basketball game, when you...fainted. I'd been taping you and you were playing with your necklace then. It caught my eye because it seemed very familiar to me, like I'd seen it before."

"I've to go," I said. "I'm going to miss my ride."

"Oh, I think he'll wait for you."

"Really, I need to go." I could feel something bad was about to happen. Something very bad.

"I think you're going to want to hear what I have to say," he said.

I stopped and waited. "I'm all ears," I said, but I wasn't. In my mind I was plotting my escape.

"Anyway, after I got a still of you at the game, I blew up a portion of your necklace and your hand twisting it and with your hair just so covering your face. And you know what I found by searching with that image? Do you?"

My mind was racing. He couldn't have known.

"I found dozens of images of a girl just like you. Your height, your hair color...your necklace. I couldn't make out her face, though, because she was always covering it with her hair. Do you know what girl I'm talking about, Laney?"

"Why are you doing this?"

"I should've found this out sooner, but your mother changed her last name when you moved and that stumped me. That kid, West, he was your brother, wasn't he? The murderer? He was the one who killed all of those people on that bus. Wasn't he?"

"Shut up," I said.

Craig said. "You can either give me a comment on it now or not. Either way I'm going to hit send on it right about now." He held out his tablet and hit the screen.

I pushed away from him. Maybe he was bluffing. I turned from my locker and went to the library instead. I got online and found Craig's post. There, as promised, he'd published a piece about Marshall and me—about how cozy we looked, but then he edited the piece and added links to a bunch of stories about West and Mark, speculating about my involvement, linking to the pictures of me in the newspapers around the country. I saw white dots spinning and swirling before my eyes. Already, there were comments. Kids were wondering if I was involved and if I was a terrorist. They said that they thought there was something weird about me. That I was quiet and that I lived with the crazy old hermit. Then they suggested that maybe she was a terrorist, too. "Maybe we should burn their house down," someone wrote. "Maybe we should have them arrested, or maybe we should kill them," said another. All anonymously.

It was all over. I took the back stairs from the library, not sure where to go next.

I headed down the hall, when I saw Marshall. He walked toward me. I couldn't ever talk to him again. I turned and ran. I didn't even know where I was going. I ran through the halls and up and down the stairs. I ran until I was in front of Mrs. Ringly's office, banging on the door. "Let me in," I said, "please let me in."

•

After Mrs. Ringly calmed me down and got me to tell her what happened, she assured me that the story would be taken down immediately and that Craig would be in big trouble. "No," I said, "please don't punish him. Please just leave it alone. I deserve it. I deserve everything they're saying about my family and me. I'm the one who should be punished. It was stupid of me to ever think I could be normal."

"Laney," she said. We sat next to each other on a small couch. She took my hand in hers the way a mother would. "You did nothing wrong."

"I did everything wrong," I said. "I should've stopped him. I should've saved them."

"Did you know what your brother was going to do?" she said. I shook my head.

"Then what could you have done?"

"I could've been a better sister to him."

"I'm sure you were a great sister," she said.

"I wasn't," I said, and then I admitted something I'd never admitted to myself. "I didn't like West very much anymore. He was mean to me. He scared me. I just wanted him to go away."

"It's not your fault, Laney," she said. But no matter how many times she said it, all I could think of was what Marshall's face was going to look like when he found out the truth about me. He would look just as disgusted and repulsed as those other people.

Mrs. Ringly agreed to drive me home again. She said she'd like to talk to Meme but I told her no, it was okay. When we got to Chellie's driveway, she kept insisting, but also looking at her watch. She had somewhere to go. "Really," I said. "I'm fine."

"I'm going to have to get in touch with your social worker, Laney," she said. "It's policy."

"Whatever," I said. "It's cool." It didn't matter now. Let Marta come and take me away. She could send me wherever she wanted to now. The North Pole. No matter where they sent me, I would never be safe. Someone would always find out about me.

"Okay," she said. "I'll leave you here, but I'll be back in touch with you tomorrow. We'll figure this out." She smiled at me. I smiled back but I was only pretending. There was nothing to figure out. My time here was done.

I watched her drive away and then I headed out onto the ice. The days were getting longer, the snow softer. Soon the ice would begin to soften as well. I needed to find my way from here before too long.

I followed Marshall's tracks and was making good progress, but then the pressure started up. Not now. I needed to move. The pressure became so strong that it brought me to my knees.

I was on my knees and she was on the floor in front of me, bleeding already, terrified. My mother. "You don't need to do this, West. Please. Let me help you." Even though I'd already cut her she still looked at me with love. Why? Why? Stop loving me. Stop loving me. Can't you see how dark it is inside of me? Can't you see how ugly I am? Can't you see how much I hate you? Now you can feel my pain.

I raised my hand with the knife in it and she flinched. "Please, West," she begged. "Please, just don't hurt Laney. Please don't hurt Laney. I'm begging you." She shut her eyes and whispered please over and over. Up above I heard a helicopter. It was time to find Laney.

I felt the cold beneath my knees, but not from the cold. My mother begging for my life. No longer worried about her own. She only worried about me.

My heart pushed against this body cage. It roared to get out of me. There was too much for it to hold. My mother. My mother.

I needed to get to the safety of the trees. I got up and ran. I stumbled and my foot broke through. Snow filled up my boot. I had to stop and empty it, even though I couldn't afford to waste time.

I heard a sled in the distance. I was up and running again. Soon, Marshall caught up to me. He circled around to stop, but I headed off in the other direction. "Leave me alone," I yelled, but he kept coming. Off his sled, he ran after and tackled me. We lay panting on the snow. "Go away," I said. I thought of how we'd been there, in nearly that same exact place, just a few days before—it had all been perfect then. Now everything was ruined.

"Laney," he said.

"I'm disgusting," I said.

"What your brother did is not you."

"How would you know?" I said.

"He made his own choice," he said. "You're a good person, Laney." I was annoyed that he had said such a mature, even-keeled thing. He had no idea what I'd witnessed, what I'd lived through. West was still a part of me. We shared the same blood. With every vision, I was becoming more and more like him. I felt him everywhere. I felt my mother's blood on my hands. My mother.

"I wish he'd just killed me," I said, which had been the wish deep inside me all along. If only he had killed me that night, then I would be one of the victims instead of someone to blame after the fact. "Why didn't he just kill me? She begged for him not to hurt me. My mother begged for my life as she was dying. Why did she do that? Why didn't he just kill me?"

"I'm so glad he didn't," Marshall said.

"I'm a disaster."

"None of us are perfect," he said.

"You are," I said. My mind flashed back to the visions I'd had of him. His anguish over his father saying that there was something wrong with him.

"I have to tell you something. You might not like it."

"You can tell me anything," I said. "I'll still like you no matter what."

"That's what I'm afraid of, too, Laney," he said. "How you like me."

"Because of Linda?"

"Linda's my friend," he said. "My best friend."

"And your girlfriend?"

"Not anymore," he said. Nothing else mattered then. Not West. Not the victims in the sky. Nothing. "We used to be together a long time ago, but now we're just friends."

"Is she angry at me because of what Craig said?"

"Not at you," he said. "She's angry at me. She thinks I'm not being fair to you." He still had me pinned down on the ground. I pushed him up and off me. He stood up. "My father hates me," he said quietly. "He kicked me out of the house this morning. I have nowhere to go."

"Why would anyone hate you?"

Marshall sat down in the snow and sobbed. I put my arm around him.

"It's okay," I said. "You can talk to me."

"Laney, it's just that… "

He took a deep breath. "It's just that my father found out something about me and hates me now."

"What? What did he find out?"

"I can't tell you," Marshall said.

"That's not fair," I said. "You know every horrible thing about me and you can't tell me this one thing?"

"I'm sorry," he said again. "I'm sorry."

The sky spiraled down into a pinprick, into one snowflake hurtling towards me like a spear. I broke free of him and ran as fast as I could. He didn't follow me.

I left him there alone. He had nowhere else to go and I left him there alone.

It was nearing the end of March and warmer every day. The lake was getting too dangerous to cross. I wouldn't have crossed even if I could. I was never going back to that school again. Mrs. Ringly had gotten in touch with Meme. "Children are nothing but animals,"

Meme said. "And that's insulting to animals, actually. Never mind about them. They don't matter anyway. All that matters is what's right here on this bluff." I was starting to think maybe she was right. Maybe it was better to keep yourself away from society. To become a hermit. I still hadn't forgiven her for what she'd said about my mother, but I would stay with her for now, until the days became warmer and I made my escape.

Every day I was having more and more visions, but not of Meme or Alice, all of them of West, scribbling in his book, sharpening his knife, readying himself. I was reliving his preparations. His excitement and fear. It was excruciating. I couldn't risk being around people all day, as each time the visions made me appear to lose consciousness. I was enough of a freak as it was. I burned with shame at the thought of seeing Marshall again. He'd probably been laughing at me all along, but I worried over him, too, and wondered where he was living. I was furious at him for not telling me his secret after everything he knew about me—like he didn't trust me. And furious at myself for leaving him alone on the ice.

I both wanted to see him again and didn't want to see him. Didn't matter either way because Chellie was going to bring me my homework now. Meme had set it up without my knowledge. Other than seeing her, I'd be alone with Meme until the lake opened up and I could take a boat across. Escape was still an option. I'd find a way to be rid of all them all. Maybe I would trek up to Canada and cross the border, begin life where no one knew me.

When I asked her why I couldn't just take the path out, she said, "To what? There's no car waiting for you. There's no paved road. It's a rough trip. Not for frivolous young girls who are used to living in big cities. You'd get yourself lost out there."

"I know how to use my snowshoes now and my compass," I reminded her.

"You're still too soft," she said. I could tell she didn't really believe that. She wanted to keep me close.

She knew nothing about me. We never lived in big cities, just small towns where I spent most of my time outdoors, like I did on the bluff. I was getting to know these woods. I thought I could make it on the path. Someday I would try. I was learning all the time about the woods and how to maneuver in the wild. I knew more than she thought I did.

But I waited. For the end of the day, when I could go to sleep. For each morning, when I could wake up so that I might wait for sleep again.

Each day, I thought of Marshall. No matter what, I still loved him and I thought just maybe I could make him love me back. If only he would tell me his secret. If only I would see him again.

I spent as much of my days outside as possible. I listened, as Meme said, to the lake. When it was ready to start breaking up it would groan and screech. "You'll know it when you hear it," she said.

I heard nothing but the chickadees and, up the shore, a pileated woodpecker knocking on an old stump of a tree.

If I could have, I would have melted the lake with my mind.

I listened and heard the birds, the wind, and a car honking across the lake, over there where people lived. Over there where Marshall was living a life that did not include me. My eyes still looked to the north when I thought of him.

I walked a path I was familiar with, one which led down to the shore and then along the edge of the bluff, headed to the south. In front of me was the lake, looking as frozen as ever, though the snow had softened even more and so, I assumed, had the ice beneath. Ahead were mountains leading to mountains, hushed and blue beneath the cloudless sky. Then I saw them, tracks unlike others I had seen before. These were not deer, or fox, or squirrel—they were bird. Lots of them. I got down on eye-level with the tracks and looked closely. I stood and trained my mind to view the scene from above as though I were flying. Below me I saw the tops of pine trees, leafless maples, I saw snow, white and cold, and I saw a circle of tracks, leading on.

Back on the ground I followed, slowly, quietly. Before long, I saw them in the distance—a flock of turkeys, dark and still against the white snow. One of the birds stretched out its wings, turned its head and noticed me. He alerted the others and they raced off, heads forward.

I wanted to let them know I wouldn't hurt them. I'm a peaceful observer, I would've said if I spoke their language, but I didn't and so they were gone as though they had never been there to begin with. All that was left were their tracks, melting in the snow, ready to be obliterated by the sun, by wind, by time.

I found a stump near the shore and sat down, quieted my breath. I felt strongly that I had been here before in this spot. I shut my eyes and willed a vision.

I was there, in that spot. It was summer, warm, wind. I heard children's voices, laughing. And a woman's voice. Alice. There she was at the water's edge, beautiful. Her long hair shining. She turned and smiled at me. "Come on," she said. "The kids are swimming."

I stood up from the stump and walked down to them. My family. Alice was in cut off shorts that showed off her long, tanned legs. I waded into the water and stood next to her, put my arm around her shoulders. She rested her head against me. "I love you," she said, and I felt her love wrap up into me. "Look at them," she said, nodding in direction of the kids. My children. My babies.

They were all that was the best of us, her and me. West noticed us then and grinned, picked up his pail full of water and made to splash us with it. The baby, Laney, giggled with fright as I made my way toward them, pretending to be a scary monster. "No, Dada," she said. "No. No."

I came to and could tell by the light that not much time had passed. My father. He was there and loved us once. We'd been a family. A real family. But it had all gone wrong. I felt something in that vision that I'd never known before: what it means to belong to something larger than yourself. What it means to care for others more than you do yourself. What it means to love.

Thursday and it was raining outside. Steady and dull thump, thump, rattle on the roof. It was good to have rain, I had to remind myself. Rain would help the melt.

Meme was working on her project and because I was bored, I sat down to help her. After a few hours of sorting photos, she handed me a stack of letters. "These might interest you," she said.

I flicked through the envelopes. They were all addressed to my mother. They were all from Ben, my father.

"Why do you have these?" I asked. These letters were not hers.

"She left them when she left here," Meme said, sorting, sorting, sorting. "Just like she left her other things." Not looking up. "It was like she wanted to leave as much of her past behind her as she could—not that I can blame her about that."

"Why are you giving them to me?" I asked.

"It's time you learned the truth," she said. There were such a few of them. I held them in my hand and weighed them, ounces. I wished they had been more substantial. This was my history I held in my hand. My roots.

There were five letters total. All from an Air Force base in Georgia. "He was far from home," I said.

"Yes. They thought even the government had it in for them. They believed that no one wanted them to stay together. I'll admit I did try to keep them apart before you kids came along, but they just kept finding a way to each other. They were magnetized to each other."

I looked at the letters, the careful script. I read them chronologically. The first one was dull. He misses her. He misses us kids. He wants to come home to us and be a real family. He talks of his days—boot camp, training. He talks of the men he has met. He misses so much. He misses and misses.

The second one was shorter. He thanks her for the package. He loves the photos of the kids.

The third one said, *"Screw you, Alice. Why don't you just divorce me then and get it over with? You're the one who wanted the kids and now all you can do is bitch about how they never get to see their daddy. What do you want me to do? This is my job."*

In the fourth one, he apologizes and reassures her that he loves her and trusts her. He tells her that she is his soul mate. He tells her he can't live without her.

"I have a hard time breathing here," he said in one letter, *"without you near me. I wish I could absorb you into my body and that we could live as just one person instead of two."*

The fifth letter was downright scary. He rants that he knows what she's done. Knows what she's up to. He says that he is aware that she and her mother are against him and he'll be damned if they'll get away with it. *"I'm coming to get you, Alice,"* he said. *"Don't think you can stop me."*

I looked up from the letter and Meme was watching me.

"He came back here," she said.

"What happened?"

"He left his barracks and came home. He was AWOL, but they just discharged him anyway because of his mental state."

"What was wrong with him?"

"I don't know what they would call it now exactly. His head wasn't right. I'm just not sure, Elane." Her face looked older, more tired. She rubbed her cheeks with her fingers. "Apparently, he got worse when he was a teenager and then there was Alice. He tried to break it off but that was only temporary. He was obsessed with her. It was unhealthy. I worried for her safety. I worried what he might do to her when he was off his medication. When he was on it, he was fine, but he needed help. He really did." She sighed and looked out the window. "I thought it would be okay if I just kept them apart."

"But they loved each other," I said.

"They were too young and stupid to know anything about love. Especially Alice. If only they'd listened to me."

If only they'd listened to her, I would never have existed, but then neither would West.

"You're wrong," I said. "They knew a lot about love."

"How would you know?" she asked, looking at me suspiciously. I felt almost as though she could read my mind, or that she knew about the visions.

"I just know," I said. "I feel it."

These letters didn't belong to her and her stupid project. They didn't even really belong to me. They belonged to my mother alone. I left the room, away from her and her eyes.

But once she'd opened her mouth, she couldn't contain the story. She followed me wherever I went so that she could unburden herself. I was lying in my bed with the covers pulled up to my chin. She sat on the edge of the bed with her back to me, talking on.

He came home. Alice was living with her, and so were we kids. It was easiest with him away. She and us kids couldn't follow until he'd made it through his basic training and been assigned somewhere. This made Meme happy. She thought if she could keep Alice here, she might convince her to stay, and then she'd be safe.

"So he left and not soon after, he came home. He was thin," she said. "Lost fifteen or twenty pounds off his already thin frame. He looked hollowed out. He looked like he was dying."

He came home on a day when the sky was pelting down freezing rain. We were all sitting around the fire, West and I playing with blocks, while Meme and Alice worked on a quilt. Though Alice had been bitter about staying behind at first, she'd fallen into a rhythm once again with her mother. It was better for everyone that they were there, especially the kids. As much as she loved Ben, she felt content in the warm cozy room right then. She didn't want to be anywhere else. Ben's letters had scared her, thrown her off kilter. She didn't know whether to tell her mother about them or not. Eventually, she had decided to share them with her mother, share her fear.

The last thing they expected was for my father to enter the room, though they had spoken of what they would do if he returned. They had made an emergency plan together. That's how it had gotten between the two of them. They'd joined together to protect the children and each other.

"You're home," Alice said, and jumped up to greet him. Meme stood up, too, as West and I called out *Daddy, Daddy* and reached for him. "His eyes were all wrong," she said. "They were hard and unfocused. They were like ice."

He made nice for a bit and hugged us kids and let everyone fawn over him. Then he shooed West and me out of the room to let into Meme and Alice.

"I've had you two watched," he said. "I know what you've been up to. I know you're both plotting against me." In a way they felt guilty, because they had joined forces against him, but not out of malice, out of protection. "We questioned our own sanity, then, I think," Meme said. "Had he had someone watch us? Were we doing the right thing in protecting ourselves against him?"

Then he said that which is impossible to consider. He told them they would not take his children away. No one would. "Wherever I go, the kids go," he said. "I'm taking them, and there's not a thing you can do about it."

Meme tried to reason with him. She'd known men like this. Alice's own father, long gone, had been such a man. "Oh, the patterns we fall into in our lives. This is why I knew he wasn't right for her from the start. I'd lived it myself," Meme said. Alice tried to reason with him. They were trapped. Finally, that night when he slept, Meme said to Alice, "Go now. Take the kids. Get them to safety." It was as they had planned.

Alice asked if she should call the police. Meme told her no. "I'll deal with him," she said. "Don't worry."

Alice left with us in the night. This must be what I remember—walking across the lake in the night. It was late winter, like now, the ice softening, but her fear of Ben must have been larger than her fear of us all falling through.

She made it to the other side, to Chellie, where we waited.

That night the ice groaned and screeched and wailed. It was so loud that it woke him up. He went looking for us kids and confronted Meme. He told her he would kill her if she didn't say where we had gone.

"They took to the lake," she said, and then she pointed him in the direction we left. But she had lied—and my memory had lied. We had left by the path, not the lake. The lake was melting, breaking up. No sane person would have chosen to cross that lake.

Ben walked out onto the lake. The last time Meme saw him he was heading out toward the center, a low fog building up all around him. The ice moaned and smacked.

The fog covered him over and then he was gone.

It was another week or so before the ice went out and they were able to find his body. By then, Alice had taken us and left town for good. Meme was left here, waiting for the ones she loved to come home.

"She knew what I'd done," Meme said. "She said she'd never forgive me, and she kept her word."

I looked at my hands. They were shaking.

"Can you forgive me?" she asked. Meme had sent my father out onto the melting ice. Instead of helping him get better, she sent him to his death.

I answered her as honestly as I could. I said, "I don't know."

•

When Meme left me alone finally to digest what I had heard, I tried to close my eyes and push it all away. There were too many answers and too many questions to pull together. I didn't know where to turn. I wondered what West had remembered, what he had known. I sought his insight in THE BOOK OF WEST:

All I have are scraps of memories of my dad. He lifts me into the air and tosses me up and up and up. I feel like I'm floating there until I land again in his strong hands. He holds my hand along the lakeshore and teaches me to skip a flat rock. In the evening, I sit on his lap in the rocker and listen for the call of the loon, echoing across the loneliness. Will I ever stop missing him?

We'd been stupid all these years, West and me, thinking that we'd once had a father who cared about us. No one cared. We'd been alone. Always.

I closed my eyes and waited for a vision because I knew one was coming. The pressure was there, the electricity crept across my skin. Who would it be this time? All I had to do was wait.

Cold. My feet crunched on ice. I knew it was not thick enough. I called for them. "Alice! Kids! Come back." She told me they'd taken to the lake, but that was wrong. They shouldn't have. It was too dangerous. "Alice!" I screamed. I was getting angry. How could she do this? She was risking their lives. She was a horrible mother. I should have known she would be. Neglectful and negligent. She was evil. No, she was good. I was evil. So confused. My mind was everywhere. Back and forth. No answer seemed to be the right answer.

"Come back," I screamed again. I needed them near me. I needed her near me and far away all at the same time. I had to protect her. I saw something in the distance move on the lake. It was them. It must be. I ran forward, faster now, my feet slipping in the slush. I had to get to them before the ice broke through. They wouldn't know what to do if the ice broke. They would all panic, make it worse. Alice was too stupid to know to stay still and wait.

"I'll save you, kids," I yelled and hoped they heard me. "You

can't get away from me, Alice," I yelled. "I will always look for you."
I was not scared. I would be protected against harm, as I always had
been. I got to the point where I thought they were and found nothing.
I stopped and waited, listened. There, up ahead, more movement. I
took a step forward and broke through to nothing.

The ice cracked apart and my body slipped under into the frigid
water, but I felt nothing but calm. They were down there with me,
my family. I reached for them and we formed a circle with our ringed
hands. We were home at last. I was no longer afraid.

I suppose there was comfort in knowing that my father died
believing that we were all together in a beautiful way. The reality,
though, was that we were fractured and splintered and cast to the
wind. Now they were all gone.

I was the one who remained, back here at the place where
it began, the root of all evil. It was my job to stop it. To reverse
the patterns and create a new path. The only problem was that I
was weak and lacked the bravery necessary to begin again. I was
tired, and the thought of dying as my father had seemed strangely
appealing to me in that moment. I would just have to walk out on
the ice and float away.

The difference was that I would be chasing nothing, and I
would know that I was alone.

I'd been alone for all my life and didn't want that anymore.
I wanted to be a part of something bigger than myself. I wanted
to connect. I wanted to love and be loved. I wanted family and
belonging any way I could get it—and I would get it. I wouldn't
stop until I did.

Nine

It was Friday and there were candles lit on the table. We were waiting for Chellie to arrive. I was almost looking forward to it because things had been weird between Meme and me. I didn't know how to feel about her anymore. I didn't know what she would do to me. She'd practically murdered my father. My mother had never forgiven her for it, and maybe I shouldn't either.

There was a knock on the door, boots stomping, shaking off snow. Meme let Chellie in, but she wasn't alone. Marshall was there. It was almost as though I were seeing West or Ben again—as though they had come back to life and come back to me. I felt like all of the pieces of me were stitching back together. I would not survive this love.

"What're you doing here?" I asked.

"I invited him," Meme said. "It's to say thank you for all of his travels across the lake. Come in." She ushered them in and Marshall stood near me. I breathed him in, his breath like cold, fresh air. He handed me a bag of my homework.

Meme told him to sit and he did, but across from me, not beside me. It was awkward being across from him and knowing that he could see me.

Soon we were eating and Chellie and Meme were monopolizing the conversation. As usual, they were discussing their shared past. Their unshared past. Names of people I was expected to know were thrown out and laughed over or gawped at. I was beyond listening. Instead, I used my mind to send messages to Marshall. He kept his head down and ate. I had no idea if he understood what I was saying to him, which was this: tell me your secret.

After dinner, I washed the dishes and Marshall dried them. I was able to pass on my message to him then. I had written for him to come outside with me on a scrap of paper. He read it and nodded.

When Meme wasn't watching, we snuck out and ran down to the shoreline.

"Are you coming back to school?"

"I don't think so," I said.

"I'll make sure no one gives you crap," he said.

I moved toward him. I wanted to be in his arms and I hoped that this would be the time he would kiss me and tell me his secret. I'd imagined what it would feel like, so different from that time with Mark. That horrible time.

I tilted my head up to him. I knew I could make him love me. I knew I could.

"Laney," he said. "Please. I can't." He didn't sound irritated or disgusted, just sad.

I stepped back.

"I'm really sorry," he said. "I should go." He turned to leave.

"Marshall, wait," I called after him. "I love you."

Meme stood on the path above us, shining a flashlight down. "I knew it," she said. Marshall stopped and turned.

"You don't understand," I said to her.

"Oh, believe me, I do understand. This is about history repeating itself and we'll have no more of that. Not while I'm still living. You're not welcome here, young man," she said. "Don't you ever come back."

"It's not what you think," Marshall said.

She said, "I have a loaded rifle in the house and I'm not afraid to use it."

Marshall left then, with Meme's ugly words and my *I love you* hanging in the air between us like a soiled sheet. I was alone upstairs crying when I heard her and Chellie below. Chellie tried to calm her down, but she would have none of it. "Get in touch with that social worker and tell her to come collect her," Meme said. "I have rules and she was warned what would happen if they were broken."

"Come on," Chellie said. "They're kids."

"I'm aware what kids are capable of," Meme said. "Fully aware."

"Give Laney another chance," she said. "She's good for you."

"Oh, is that what this is about? You want her here so you don't have to worry about me? Well, forget it. And forget worrying about me. I can take care of myself."

"Nadine," she said. "We both know you need help."

"I need nothing," Meme said. "I don't need you. I don't need her. And I most certainly don't need help. Now you get out of here before I use that rifle on you."

Chellie tried to talk, but Meme wouldn't listen. Then she, too, finally left. I waited and waited for Meme to come upstairs and scream at me or kill me or do whatever she was going to do, but instead there was only silence inside and the wailing of the shrinking ice outside.

The next morning, I didn't know what to do, so I packed up my bags and sat on my bed and waited. I wasn't sure if Marta would be coming for me, or if Meme would send me to her. I wasn't sure if I wanted to leave or stay. Where would I go now? Where would I be safe and free? I couldn't think of another place I could live. The bluff felt like my home now. I knew it.

I listened to Meme moving around downstairs, mumbling to herself. Slamming cabinets. Rustling paper. Finally, I heard her pull on her boots and jacket and leave for a walk without saying anything.

I ran downstairs and stuffed some food and drink in my mouth, used the bathroom, brought a few snacks with me upstairs and went back up to my bed, the only place that felt like it might be mine.

Hours went by. I tried to read my tracking book while I waited for her, but I couldn't focus. I opened THE BOOK OF WEST instead:

I'm excited mostly, but sometimes I'm scared, too. What if there is nothing after I die? What if there is only blackness and nothing else? What if I don't even know that there is only blackness? I feel just the same as I felt the very first time I ever really looked at the night sky. I was with my father. He brought me out special to see the northern lights. He didn't wake Alice or Laney because he said it was just between us guys. At first I was scared of how they looked, but then as my dad talked about them and told me they wouldn't hurt me, I started to see how beautiful they were. I asked him where they came from. I said, "Did God make them?" and he said he wasn't sure. Maybe, he said. Maybe. Then he said, if that's what you want to believe, it's okay to believe that. I wanted to believe it. I wanted to believe there was a god who would take care of us. A god who would be there when we died to comfort us.

Now I'm not so sure.

I wished he would've known that it was okay to be unsure and scared. I wished he would've known that being lonely isn't the end of the world. I wished he would've known all of the things I'd learned since I'd been here living in this woods—all of the beauty, and the hard work, and the quiet northern sky. I wished he would've known that there was more to look forward to in life. If only he had known what it felt like to be in love. Even when it hurt, being in love was better than hurting other people and being dead, I was sure of that now. I wished he would've known that hurting other people will not take away your own pain. I wished he would've known that hurting other people only turns your pain into an even bigger and uglier wound that rips a hole in the sky.

I looked at my watch. It'd been three hours since she left. Winter was passing, but it was still cold out and she had never been gone for so long before. I tried to call up a vision of her, of where she might be, but nothing came to me. I was scared for her. She'd seemed different lately, more scattered, less sharp. I might not have agreed with everything she did, and I was definitely still angry with her for what she'd said, but she was my grandmother. If she was hurt out there or lost, I needed to find her. She was all I had. I became consumed with the idea that she needed me. It was in my gut. I was starting to believe that my gut knew a thing or two and I should listen to it.

Outside, I searched for her tracks. I crouched down low. The ground was part snow and part mud now, so I had to be careful to not lose her trail. She started at the shoreline and then took to the woods. I found myself in an area I'd not yet explored—the back of the bluff in what looked like a protected cove. And there I lost the trail.

Sweat broke out beneath the band of my woolen cap. The sun was high now and nothing looked as I remembered it. A twig cracked and snow tumbled down. I stopped to listen. Nothing. I started walking, though I knew I shouldn't have. I was determined to find her, but the farther I walked, the less familiar the landscape looked. I was used to it in winter, with snow cover, but now the melt had changed the place.

I was angry with myself for thinking I knew anything about tracking. Meme was lost, and now I was, too. I sunk to my knees on a crusty patch of snow and pushed my gloved fingers into my eyes. If only I had not lost her trail. Where was she? Where?

The pressure pushed in through my temples with a force I hadn't expected.

I was in this spot but it was later in spring, some leaves on the trees. I heard the white-throated sparrow's song pierce through the woods. I had my hand on my pregnant belly. I pushed through branches, stumbled over roots. The path was clear. Through some bushes, I came to a small clearing, the foundation of a house. I counted four chimneys. The house must have been glorious. It had burned fifty years earlier. I had only seen it in photos. It had been my dream to live in such a house one day. I stopped in the middle of the foundation. "You and I will build this house together, Alice," I said out loud, hands rubbing my belly.

The vision shrank down to a pinprick in my brain and faded out. I stood up and followed the path she had taken all those years before, pregnant Meme with my mother in her belly. I pushed through some low pines and I heard her talking. She was just past one of the chimneys, sitting on a rocky ledge that would have once been a wall.

"Alice? Is that you?" she said. I walked over to her, careful not to surprise her.

"Meme," I said, "Are you okay?"

"Please don't leave again, Alice." Meme was looking at me when she spoke. She thought I was my own mother. She said it with such conviction that I wondered if I was her. Had she invaded my body through one of my visions? I looked down. My hands were still my own. They were girl hands. My hands.

"Do you forgive me?" she asked.

"Yes," I said, not bothering to correct her. "I forgive you." And I meant it. I did forgive her. What she had done was horrible but she was beyond that now.

I said, "Will you come with me?" I took her hand and she surprised me by gripping it back.

"I missed you," she said. "I'm so glad you're home."

"I'm glad to be home," I said. She stood up and pulled me to her. She was crying. I started crying, too, but I didn't know why. I only knew that it felt good to finally cry.

I cried for my mother.

I cried for my grandmother.

I cried for my father.

Most of all, I cried for West's victims, their beautiful lives cut short, each becoming a swirl of light in the sky above me. I cried for them the most. I would've done anything to bring West's victims back to life. I would've given my own life for theirs.

Then, I cried for Marshall, alone and scared.

Finally, I cried for myself.

She let me lead her home and get her warmed up by the fire. When I had gotten some food into her, I helped her to bed and wrapped her in blankets.

We lay next to each other on her bed. Meme had her hands folded across her chest. Dark was coming and the stars twinkled in through the window. She'd been so quiet, I thought that she might be asleep, but she said, "These scraps of paper and cards and envelopes and photos left behind tell a story about the people who left them. You could tease out someone's whole life from a couple of photograph albums and some shopping lists. What could you learn about me from my memory books?"

"I don't know," I said.

"You're a curious girl. Come on. What would you want to know?"

"I guess I'd want to know how you ended up here living like this." It was something I'd wondered about for a long time, but was too afraid to ask. Something had broken down between us now. Nothing seemed off limits.

"My heart had always been here," she said. "It was our summer place, and my mother and I spent every June through August throughout my childhood. They were great summers." She stretched her arms up and moved her hands down to her belly, folded there as in prayer. "Then I grew up and got married and had Alice and didn't have time to come here anymore. Around that time my father winterized the place with insulation and installed the bathroom. Before that we had only the outhouse. That would not have suited you."

I turned on my side to watch her speak. "Daddy had planned on getting a road through and some electricity, but that never happened. He died young, heart attack, and then Mother ended up in the old folks home early because of her mind."

"What was wrong with her?"

"They called it sundowning," she said. "She would start to forget things and talk crazy towards the end of the day. I wanted to care for her myself, but my husband wouldn't let me."

"What happened to him?"

"He left me. Took off for Florida, then Nevada. He married another woman and had two girls, even though we never officially divorced. He died. Apparently he was up in a hot air balloon for some publicity stunt for his business and something went awry. Can you believe that? Alice didn't know her father much. Just as well, I guess."

"After he left and my parents were gone, this was the only safe place I knew. Alice was different, a challenging child and difficult young woman. She needed protecting, I thought. I brought her here because I believed that I could save her, but instead I ruined her. You can't protect someone who doesn't want protecting. When she got pregnant, I felt ashamed that I had created such a damaged child. I'd not done right by her. What would people think? And then when your father came back, I should have chosen a different course. The course I chose only fueled West's anger all these years later. He knew. Your brother knew how your father died. Your mother told him. She wrote me one Christmas to tell me. 'He knows it's your fault, Mother,' she said. 'He knows what you did.' By that point she'd left me for good, only writing once a year if I was lucky. I could never keep track of your whereabouts, my cards and letters returned to sender because you'd moved on. I was in hell without you. If only I could have been there. I know I could have stopped West. I know it."

It was the first time she had acknowledged his wrongdoing.

"The blood of those people is on my hands, Elane. It all starts and ends with me."

"West was sick and needed help," I said. "He did this to himself. If you're to blame, then I am, too."

"I could have helped him," she said. "I should have."

"How would you have helped him?" I looked at her, but she would not meet my eyes.

"I think you know how, Elane," she said, and finally looked at me. Her eyes pierced through mine and into my brain. She knew.

"The visions," I said.

"Yes," she said. "I gave them to you."

"How? Why?"

"My mother gave them to me many years ago before she passed and I hadn't planned on giving them to anyone else. I wanted them to die with me. I always believed they were like a curse."

"Why would you do this to me?"

"Laney, I gave them to you so that they might save you."

"Save me?"

"After West—after what happened with West, after the horrible, vile things he did—I realized that had I been able to give the visions to him when he was younger, he might have learned more about why people do the things they do. He might have learned how to see other people as the flawed and beautiful creatures they are. He might have felt something for somebody other than himself. Empathy, I mean. He might have learned to make better choices."

There was some truth to what she said. I'd learned things

about my mother and father—and about her—that had changed my mind about nearly everything. I'd also learned things about West, horrible things, that only made his actions more confusing and disturbing. Perhaps there was no way to understand what he did, just as there was no way to forgive it.

"Why didn't you give them to him?"

"He was like Alice—never strong enough to handle them. The two of them loved too easily and too quickly. They were not resilient. Their guard was always down."

"West never loved anyone," I said. "He hated. I've seen it in his own words. I've felt it."

"That's not true, Laney. He loved you all very deeply, but he was damaged. Sometimes love and hate become confused and a desire to possess becomes too strong to manage, and out of that desire comes rage. He was weak, but you, you are strong. You are brave. The women are the keepers of the vision in our family. From now on, it's up to you. When you're ready, it will be your responsibility to pass the vision on, or to let it die with you."

"Why didn't you let it die?"

"I wanted you to live. I wanted you to know love and not succumb to bitterness. From birth we could see that your brother was different—that he had absorbed what his father and mother passed onto him. That is the yin and yang of our family. Our curse and our blessing. But then there was you, Laney—so obviously light. Even in your darkness, the light shines through. I could not let you fade away. So I made the choice to pass the vision on to you, and then my own memory started to fade, just like my mother's had. It's the loss of the vision. Once it's gone, all of the memory you've stored up starts to fade away, giving strength to the new keeper of the vision," she said. "I was too scared to give them to you sooner. I thought they would hurt you as they had me, but now I see I was wrong. I'm an old lady. I've had my time. Now it's your time. But you can only use the vision for good. If you use it to harm another, there will be consequences."

"Like what?"

Meme frowned. Shook her head. "Best you just know that the consequences will be dire." She gripped my hand with her cold fingers. "Just promise me you will you the vision for good. If you have the vision, you have an opportunity to be the light in this family. To squelch the darkness."

"You're not well," I said. Meme's face grew paler. "And I've got to find help for you. Can you tell me the way out of here?"

"There's a path through the north-facing trees. Stick along the shore and you'll find the old logging road. Take that out to the skidoo club and use the key beneath the mat. There's a phone inside. Call Chellie."

I left her there, warm beneath the covers, and followed her instructions to the phone. Chellie said she would come right away.

"She stayed here for you, Laney," she said to me before he hung up. "The doctor wanted her in the hospital, but she wanted to be with you."

When Chellie arrived, she filled me in. Meme was sick. Her dementia had gotten worse. She shouldn't have been living alone, but she wanted to have this time with me. She had planned to move to town, but risked her life and health by staying there with me.

All my life I'd thought everyone had taken from me, only to learn they were giving to me all along. Sacrificing. I went up to Meme's bed and held her hand while she slept. "I'll never leave you," I said. "Never in a million years."

Chellie said she'd be taking her to the hospital soon. "You'll have to come with me," she said. "I can't leave you here alone. And, oh, I almost forgot," she said, "your neighbor from back home called. She said not to worry. Marta will be here soon."

Ten

Marta hollered my name as she saw me across the parking lot. She launched herself on to me and hugged until I had to push her off. We were standing outside the hospital entrance, and I was embarrassed that someone might see us.

"How are you? You've been through so much. Poor dear," she said. I pushed her away. Everything about her seemed false now. I wanted her away.

"Not like I had a lot of choice," I said.

"I'm here now to take you back," she said.

"I'm staying," I said. Marta looked at me funny. I could see she was starting to get angry, thinking me difficult. "It's Meme," I said. "She needs me."

"Your grandmother is sick. You can't stay here on your own. You're a minor. I'm responsible for you."

"She's fine," I said. "She just needs rest. Come up and meet her. You'll see."

I had coached Meme. After I explained to her and Chellie what it meant that Marta was coming, they'd both jumped on board. We would work together to help Meme to present herself to be as healthy a person as possible. "You'll have to be nice to her," I said.

"Bah," Meme scowled. "Since when does pleasant mean healthy?"

"If she doesn't buy this," I said, "then it's off to foster care for me."

"We've got this," Chellie said. "Right, Nadine?"

"We won't let that happen," Meme said.

We'd agreed that I would stay with Meme on the bluff and take care of her with Chellie's help. Her dream had been to live out the rest of her life, which might very well be a long one, on the bluff. The doctor had already given her some medicine, and if we kept her dosed properly, she might be fine for a while.

When Marta met her, Meme pulled out all the stops. She was her most charming and intelligent self, though I could tell it took a toll on her to work so hard for it. She was tired.

"Well, I think it seems like everything is in order here," Marta said. "I just need to visit with the school and make sure everything is okay there and then we'll be good." I winced. I'd forgotten about the school.

"We've been homeschooling," I said.

"Yes," Marta said, "but you're supposed to be in school once a week, yes?"

"Yes," I said. "I've just been waiting for the ice to go out." I was scrambling for something to keep her away from the school.

"I'm not following you, Laney." Marta looked troubled. She looked like she might change her mind.

"So I can get across the lake by a boat. The ice needs to be out."

"Ah, okay," she said, relieved that she could keep things as they were and not have to file any more paperwork. "That makes sense. So if I call the school next week they'll tell me you've been there, then?"

"Yes," I said. "I'll be there." She might not have been as stupid as I thought she was. She'd tricked me into going back to school, but that was okay. The way I felt right then, I would have walked across hot coals to stay with Meme on the bluff. I wanted us both to go home.

•

She'd been home for a few days and began to regain her strength. We were sitting at the table one morning eating cereal and drinking fresh-squeezed orange juice, a treat that Meme had said we deserved. She piped up and told me that I shouldn't avoid what was inevitable. "If we're going to stay here, you have to go back to school and face those kids, Laney," she said. "Show them what you're made of."

It was a Monday and the ice was out. She told me to get dressed, and then she brought me across the lake in the aluminum fishing boat and dropped me off at Chellie's, where I would catch the bus. I stood out at the road waiting, stomping my feet to keep my toes from getting cold. Spring was coming on fast. I listened hard and heard the wood thrush deep in the woods, calling out to the morning.

I looked up the road for the bus. I would climb the steps and take a deep breath and accept whatever anyone had to say to me. I would give it right back, too. I am not my brother. I have never been my brother.

A truck pulled up across from me and lowered the window. "Want a ride?" It was Marshall. I looked down at my feet. "Get in," he said. I looked both ways, crossed the road and got into his truck. The space felt both familiar and odd at the same time—a place of so much hope at one time and then it was filled with shame and embarrassment.

I had told him I loved him.

"I'm sorry about everything," he said. He didn't need to go into details. We both knew what he was talking about.

"It's okay." I looked down at my lap. I couldn't look at his eyes. I was ashamed that I'd tried to kiss him and that he'd refused me. I wasn't good enough for him. Not pretty enough. Also, he knew what was wrong with me. He knew about West. I couldn't blame him for not wanting me. "I don't blame you," I said. "I know it's hard because of what my brother did."

"It's not that, Laney."

"Sure," I said.

"I gave Craig an exclusive. I told him my story. I told him about my secret and he's posting it today. It should be on his Tumblr right now."

"You told him? Him?" Now I was angry. He'd trusted Craig and not me. "How could you do that to me?"

"I didn't do it to you," he said. "I did it for you. So you'd know about me. So everyone would."

"What would we know?"

"You'd know about how I am."

"How are you?"

"I'm gay," he said, "and proud to be."

I looked at Marshall and he nodded. He was solid and true. I didn't know what to say. It was about him and his feelings. Not because of West. Not because of me.

"It's a relief," he said. He looked genuinely happy.

"Is this why your dad was so mean to you?"

"It's been a long time since he was a father to me. I'm not sure who my family is anymore."

He told me he was staying at Chellie's house some nights and at Linda's on other nights. I looked at him as if I'd never really seen him before, as an individual with feelings. He wasn't there simply to make me feel better about himself. The love I had for him moved into something bigger than both of us. The hole my brother had left in me began to fill with the love and possibility. And family again—a new version.

"I love you, too, you know," Marshall said. "I never got a chance to say that. But I do. You're my friend." I looked out the window. The love he offered me wasn't what I hoped for, but it was what he had to give. "Can that be enough for you?" he asked. I thought about it. I thought about it hard.

"Yes," I said.

Marshall, my brother. My brother, Marshall. My friend. My

family. My home. My north.

Wherever you are, my arrow will point in your direction.

Marshall walked me into school that day with his arm around my shoulders and when Linda saw us, she linked her arm up with mine and walked beside me. Kids stared and whispered, but no one said anything mean to our faces.

We belonged. We were one, the three of us.

In homeroom, Craig stood in front of my desk. "I am sorry," he said, loud enough so that everyone, including the teacher, could hear. "Can you forgive me?" I didn't say anything, and so he whispered, "If you don't forgive me they might expel me. I can't have that on my permanent record. I want to go to college, Laney. Please."

"I'll think about it," I said, even though I had no intention of ever forgiving him. Even though everything had turned out mostly okay in the end, I still could not forget how he'd tormented me. And he didn't seem to have learned a lesson. Not really.

All day I felt a dark lump blooming within me, reaching up from my stomach into my lungs and heart until it gripped my throat, making speech nearly impossible. I went to bed early, told Meme I had a headache, but really all I wanted to do was focus hard about Craig. I lay on my bed and trained my mind on him. I was getting better at calling up the vision whenever I needed it, but still all that I saw was of the past and not the future. Meme had warned me the last time I talked to her that to use the future vision one must have come to full power. "It could take years," she said, "before you are able to see the future. And even then, you must use it sparingly for as powerful as it is, it is also dangerous." She would not or could not elaborate when I asked.

Soon the pressure began and I was in a room as darkness fell. *I was alone and the house was quiet, cold. I was hungry and so*

I went to the kitchen and opened the refrigerator though I knew there was nothing in it I wanted to eat. A bottle of ketchup and a tub of margarine. Some pickles. My mother was out, working or drinking, I wasn't sure which.

I slammed the fridge shut and sat down at the table and looked down at my schoolbooks. My name was written across the top of one of my binders: Craig Silver.

Inside the book was an official letter from MIT regarding their young scholar summer program. If you got into that program while you were still in high school, you would be a shoe in for acceptance upon graduation.

"Dear Mr. Silver," it said, "Though we appreciate your circumstances and your fine academic records, we cannot at this time offer you a scholarship position in our summer training program…"

The letter went onto to say that while they had received my academic letters of recommendation, they had not received the necessary paperwork from my guardian, despite sending her several reminder notices. My mother had forgotten to fill out the papers. She had never intended to. She herself could barely read. I was trapped in this place, living this same life she had, poor and neglectful and hating life. I was doomed. I started to cry.

I could use this information to squash him. I could torment him and wreck him and laugh all the while. I would borrow Linda's cell phone and text the news of Craig's failure to everyone in school.

I lay there for a while staring up at the ceiling, plotting Craig's downfall, but soon I stopped smiling. Meme's voice pushed into my head. The more I tried to push it away, the stronger it got: *"Use the vision only for good or the consequences will be dire."*

I didn't know what she'd meant by dire consequences. I wondered if she had ever used the vision for anything less than good. Had she faced the consequences?

I heard her voice again, *"Use the vision only for good,"* and my brain shot through with white light like a camera flash. She had done wrong with the vision. She must have. The one thing she wanted all those years ago was to keep Alice and Ben apart. She must have tried to use the vision against them but what had been the outcome?

Dire consequences.

Dire was something horrible, something disastrous. Dire was something involving great fear.

West. Of course.

Because she'd tried to use the vision to break up Alice and Ben, she faced the consequences of West being born into the darkness the same way Ben had. That's what she meant when she said it all began with her. Her actions had brought about West's darkness.

The next time I was at school, I found Craig before homeroom, standing huddled beside his locker door. "I accept your apology," I said. Tempted as I was to get revenge on Craig, I was too wary of the consequences. More importantly, though, I felt bad for him. He was alone and sad. I also realized that Craig and I now had something in common. If anyone knew what it was like to want something more than anything and to not be able to get it, it was me.

He looked up and smiled at me. "You're all right, Laney," he said.

"We've got more in common than you think we do," I said to him. I could see that we understood each other a bit better now.

Our Story Does Not End Here

The last of the ice went out in late April. Today, the lake is smooth and glassy. A perfect day for the canoe, according to Meme. She has taught me how to use a paddle, and how to listen to her commands. We pull the boat into the water and get in. One hand on the top of the paddle. The other on the body. We push forward.

We have spent much time together, alone, since she came back to the bluff. One night while we sat by the fire, she poked at the embers with a stick. I saw her as she might have been when she first came here, young and hopeful, scared. She knew my mother. She had given birth to her and she had seen inside her mind. She knew how this whole story began. "Why did she love him?" I asked her. "Do you know?"

She sighed and didn't look at me. "From the visions," she said. "It all seemed so clear at first." Sparks flew up the chimney from her poking. "They seemed to be pulled to each other." Poking. More sparks. "I think they felt as though they were on the outside of everyone else. It was exciting to finally feel understood. Everyone else thought she was this other girl—the good one, who did everything well and never made mistakes. The truth was she had to be that way. She felt she was on shaky ground living here with me. She never felt safe, and I'm sorry for that." She sat back on her chair and held up the charred end of the stick. "He saw through all of that and knew her." Meme twirled the stick like a wand.

She asked me a favor then. She wanted me to tell her more about West. I opened my mouth to speak and nothing came out. She already knew what I knew.

We knew what West was—at once beautiful and terrifying, fragile and mean. We wanted him to know how to really love, but he only believed in hate. We wanted him to be unfettered but he only knew the chains of bitterness and disappointment. West was a boy we wanted to be alive—our flesh and blood—but he had been dying inside for a really long time.

"Why am I different?" I'd waited my whole life to ask this question. I'd waited my whole life for there to be someone to answer it.

"I don't know why, Laney," she said. "I think we start to believe that our families and our genes determine who we become, but really there's something inside us that does that. Some collection of all that we know and all that we feel that molds us." She put the stick down. "Is there anything else you want to know?"

"Just one thing," I said.

Meme said, "No more secrets between us."

"Why did you go out to the woods that day?"

"Oh, well, there you go," she said. "I wish you hadn't asked me that."

"Come on," I said. "No more secrets, remember?" I knew there was something she wasn't telling me. I'd seen her in her darkest moment. I didn't want her to hide it from me.

She took a deep breath. "I went there to die, Laney. Thought you'd be better off without me, but when I saw you coming through the woods to find me, I couldn't go through with it. You need me still, just as I need you. You saved me, Laney, that day and every day that you've been here. You saved me. And now I know how wrong I would have been to leave you for good." I'd seen her in that moment of despair, when she was ready to give up her life, and I had felt her turn back toward the living. I knew she was telling the truth.

Now, she is going to show me the spot where they found Ben's body. What she doesn't know is that I know the spot as well as she does. I was there, too. But I can't tell her. The visions are mine alone now to use as I must. *"Only do good with them, Laney,"* Meme has continued to warn me. *"Only do good or you'll find that they will turn on you. A kind of karma."* Meme is trying to teach me about the visions before her memory leaves her entirely.

"Oh, that horrible, horrible night. I was terrified and alone," Meme says. "I didn't want all of you to leave. I'm not proud of what I did, sending him out here. I knew what would happen, and I can't go back and change it. All we can do is move forward. All we can do is move forward together and do better in this world."

We paddle on.

"I've been punishing myself," she says. "All these years. And then when you came back, I was terrified I'd lose you, too. I can't lose you, Laney." She looks over her shoulder at me.

"You're not going to lose me," I say.

"I didn't think I deserved you," she says.

"You do," I say, "We deserve each other."

On the way home from the hospital, I wondered if I should give her THE BOOK OF WEST to include with the rest of her books, but I decided to burn it instead and include its ashes with West's. But I kept the last page because it made me the saddest:

Today is the day! Today is the day I will be set free. No more pain. Only me and Mark and paradise. I have given up worrying about whether or not paradise exists. I know it does. It's just waiting there for me to get my revenge and come flying up to heaven. My dad will be there waiting for me and he will say, I've been waiting for you.

The lake welcomes us gently. We paddle while the waves lap against us.

"Here," Meme says, using her paddle as a rudder. "This is the spot." A swell bobs us up and over and down. I am still and quiet in the moment. Here is where my father died. His last gasp, his eyes squeezing shut. I think of him falling through the ice, reaching for us. Joining his hands with ours. I think, too, of West, his terror and regret as he walked up those bus steps. His wish to turn back. If only he had.

Turn back, West. Turn back.

I think of my mother, begging for my life. I had meant something—everything—to her. West and I both had. Even as he was killing her, she loved him. If he'd believed how strong that love was, his whole life might've been different.

If only my mother had known how much she did right. I was happy to be alive.

But now it is time to push away the futures that can never be. Now it is time to breathe fresh air into this world, to send a ripple forward for change.

I bend and pick up the two boxes. The ashes. I open the one that contains West's ashes. They are heavier than I imagined, more substantial. I open the top. The substance inside is gritty, not smooth and silky like sand. Gray. Odorless. I open the box that contains my mother.

I look up to the sky. I speak to West's victims, *Do you see this? All of you?* I lift the two boxes and pour the ashes into the lake. They swirl in the tannin-laced water before they spread and sink. *I'm letting them go.*

Clouds move in quickly. Soon it will rain, and that rain will be like the tears of West's victims, crying with relief that we have finally released them. I am crying, too.

West is gone. He is never coming back.

My mother is gone. She is never coming back.

And here I am again, a brand new girl. But this time, it is good to be new. Starting over.

What West did is my past. He is in my past. Not forgotten, but no longer living beside me as a ghost twin.

"*I will do everything I can to make the world better for the people you love,*" I say to West's victims, and I mean it. I will find some way to honor them.

I will live a good life.

I will live.

Because of them, I made it through the winter. Because of them, I survived and regained my will to live. Because of them, I tell this story. It is their story as much as it's mine.

Our story does not end here. This is where it really begins. Here is where I begin. The rain picks up and we paddle back toward shore. As we round the bend of the bluff, I turn once more and look at the wake our small boat has left behind us. Then I turn back around. We keep moving forward.

We head toward home.

Acknowledgments

Thank you to my editor, Andrew Scott, for helping me to turn this book into something I love. I am so proud of the book we made. Thank you for your thoughtful and intelligent insights, your keen eye, your great big heart, and your gentle soul. Thank you also to my publisher, Victoria Barrett, for her fierce intelligence and her unwavering dedication to creating an opportunity for voices like mine. I am grateful to you both for believing in this book and for believing in me.

Thank you to my agent, Penn Whaling, for her thoughtful guidance, her unending hard work, her impeccable reading skills, and her unflappable sense of humor. I could not imagine navigating the world of publishing with anyone else but you, Penn.

Thank you to my original mentor and great friend, Ann Blaisdell Tracy, who first opened my eyes to this writing life. Thank you to my dear friend Ellen Meister for always being available to lend her thoughtful eye and ear no matter how much she has on her plate. They broke the mold when they made you, Ellen. Thank you also to all of my other writing friends who have been cheering me on for all these years, especially Katrina Denza, Pia Ehrhardt, Pamela Erens, Kathy Fish, Kelly Flanigan, Ellen Parker, and Patricia Parkinson. Thank you to Jeff Resnick for his unflagging generosity and friendship. Thank you also to Matthew Quick and Alicia Bessette for being such beautiful friends to me. Thank you to my beloved North Country friends who always welcome me home, especially: Holly Chase, Anne Boyea, Kim Jiguere, Cathy Cook, and Jennifer Sprague. Thank you to my best friend, Caroline Ash, for all these many years of heartache and laughter. Thank you to

Maryanne Dower for being one of our family and for sharing so many Sunday nights by the fire.

Thank you to my beloved writing group for always being willing to go through the doggy door with me. Thank you, Olivia Gatti, Paul Myette, Jennifer Pieroni, and Joan Wilking. Thank you for the conversation, the commiseration, the homemade sausage, and, of course, your feedback on the first few chapters of this book was beyond compare.

Thank you to my friends at the Newbury Town Library and the Newburyport Literary festival for your commitment to literature, literacy, and community.

Thank you to my entire family. I would be lost without you all. Most of all, thank you to my husband, Allen, and my son, Henry. Allen, I love you. Thank you for giving me your heart. I cherish it and carry it with me always. Henry, everything I do is for you: from the minute I knew you were a part of me until my last breath. I will always love you.

The author is indebted to the following books, websites, and videos used as reference material in the writing of this book:

Frosty Peaks-Warm Hearts: Heritage of the Adironacks and *An Adirondack Boyhood Remembered*, both by Ralph Hoy

Mammal Tracks & Sign: A Guide to North American Species by Mark Elbroch

Dylan Klebold's Journal and Other Writings, transcribed and annotated by Peter Langman, Ph.D.

A Columbine Site—Eric Harris' Journal

Kjetil Kjernsmo's illustrated guide on how to use a compass

"The Forager's Wild Food Basics," from The Forager Press

Snowshoeing: Behind the Basics. YouTube video hosted by Amanda Beauvais

About the Author

Myfanwy Collins was born in Montreal but moved to the Adirondack Mountains in New York when she was still a child. She has since lived all over New England and worked as a waitress, a bartender, a nanny, a chambermaid, a clerk, a high school English teacher, a secretary, a ghost writer, and a traveling worker with Cirque du Soleil. She is the author of a novel, *Echolocation*, and a collection of short stories, *I Am Holding Your Hand*.

Photo credit: Olivia Gatti of Click Click Love